Y0-CZM-961

OUTNUMBERED

Taking a few steps back, Clint took a quick look around. As far as he could tell, the only threats in the area were still the three gunmen. There were some others watching from nearby buildings, but the locals already knew only too well to give Farnsworth's building a wide berth.

The first of the gunmen to make a move wasn't the one who'd done all the talking. Instead, the third man in the row made a clumsy grab for the pistol wedged underneath his belt. His hand slapped against the grip, but didn't make it any farther before Clint had drawn his modified Colt and pulled his trigger.

In that space between heartbeats, Clint had picked out his targets. All the while, he'd still been on both feet and standing in the open no more than a few paces away from the men now trying to kill him.

One more instant in that spot, and Clint knew he was a dead man . . .

DON'T MISS THESE
ALL-ACTION WESTERN SERIES
FROM THE BERKLEY PUBLISHING GROUP

THE GUNSMITH by J. R. Roberts
Clint Adams was a legend among lawmen, outlaws, and ladies. They called him . . . the Gunsmith.

LONGARM by Tabor Evans
The popular long-running series about Deputy U.S. Marshal Long—his life, his loves, his fight for justice.

SLOCUM by Jake Logan
Today's longest-running action Western. John Slocum rides a deadly trail of hot blood and cold steel.

BUSHWHACKERS by B. J. Lanagan
An action-packed series by the creators of Longarm! The rousing adventures of the most brutal gang of cutthroats ever assembled—Quantrill's Raiders.

DIAMONDBACK by Guy Brewer
Dex Yancey is Diamondback, a Southern gentleman turned con man when his brother cheats him out of the family fortune. Ladies love him. Gamblers hate him. But nobody pulls one over on Dex . . .

WILDGUN by Jack Hanson
The blazing adventures of mountain man Will Barlow—from the creators of Longarm!

TEXAS TRACKER by Tom Calhoun
Meet J.T. Law: the most relentless—and dangerous—manhunter in all Texas. Where sheriffs and posses fail, he's the best man to bring in the most vicious outlaws—for a price.

THE GUNSMITH

289

AMAZON GOLD

J. R. ROBERTS

JOVE BOOKS, NEW YORK

THE BERKLEY PUBLISHING GROUP
Published by the Penguin Group
Penguin Group (USA) Inc.
375 Hudson Street, New York, New York 10014, USA

Penguin Group (Canada), 90 Eglinton Avenue East, Suite 700, Toronto, Ontario M4P 2Y3, Canada
(a division of Pearson Penguin Canada Inc.)
Penguin Books Ltd., 80 Strand, London WC2R 0RL, England
Penguin Group Ireland, 25 St. Stephen's Green, Dublin 2, Ireland (a division of Penguin Books Ltd.)
Penguin Group (Australia), 250 Camberwell Road, Camberwell, Victoria 3124, Australia
(a division of Pearson Australia Group Pty. Ltd.)
Penguin Books India Pvt. Ltd., 11 Community Centre, Panchsheel Park, New Delhi—110 017, India
Penguin Group (NZ), Cnr. Airborne and Rosedale Roads, Albany, Auckland 1310, New Zealand
(a division of Pearson New Zealand Ltd.)
Penguin Books (South Africa) (Pty.) Ltd., 24 Sturdee Avenue, Rosebank, Johannesburg 2196,
South Africa

Penguin Books Ltd., Registered Offices: 80 Strand, London WC2R 0RL, England

This is a work of fiction. Names, characters, places, and incidents either are the product of the author's imagination or are used fictitiously, and any resemblance to actual persons, living or dead, business establishments, events, or locales is entirely coincidental.

AMAZON GOLD

A Jove Book / published by arrangement with the author

PRINTING HISTORY
Jove edition / January 2006

Copyright © 2005 by Robert J. Randisi.

All rights reserved.
No part of this book may be reproduced, scanned, or distributed in any printed or electronic form without permission. Please do not participate in or encourage piracy of copyrighted materials in violation of the author's rights. Purchase only authorized editions.
For information, address: The Berkley Publishing Group,
a division of Penguin Group (USA) Inc.,
375 Hudson Street, New York, New York 10014.

ISBN: 0-515-14056-2

JOVE®
Jove Books are published by The Berkley Publishing Group,
a division of Penguin Group (USA) Inc.,
375 Hudson Street, New York, New York 10014.
JOVE is a registered trademark of Penguin Group (USA) Inc.
The "J" design is a trademark belonging to Penguin Group (USA) Inc.

PRINTED IN THE UNITED STATES OF AMERICA

10 9 8 7 6 5 4 3 2 1

If you purchased this book without a cover, you should be aware that this book is stolen property. It was reported as "unsold and destroyed" to the publisher, and neither the author nor the publisher has received any payment for this "stripped book."

ONE

The trees were so close together that they formed a dense green curtain that nearly blocked out the sun. Branches entwined overhead and leaves brushed against one another with a sound that rivaled that of a stormy ocean when the wind was blowing just right.

The ground was covered with a thick mulch and could hardly be seen at all through the tangle of roots, fallen leaves and rooting logs. Although it couldn't be seen too well, the earth was a presence that could be smelled and touched with every move that was made.

Although he might not have been taking the time to absorb all of this, Clint was doing plenty of moving of his own. His boots stomped against the ground and nearly slipped out from beneath him with almost every step. He kept one hand in front of him as he ran, so he could push away the branches, which still managed to slap him in the face.

All around him, Clint was surrounded by a confusing mess of sounds and sights that blended into one confusing whole. Greens and browns of every shade were as easy to understand as a mess of spilled paints. He barely even had a chance to see if he was about to run into a clearing or a

1

tree trunk as his hands searched for any clue of one or the other.

Since the only way he could have been sure of where he was going was to slow down, Clint put his faith in his instincts and hoped for the best. He had never been much of a praying man, but the notion of some divine intervention right about then was getting more and more appealing.

Shots cracked through the air behind him. Lead tore through overhanging branches and punched into trees on either side. Twisting around at the waist, Clint pointed his modified Colt in the direction of the closest shooter and pulled the trigger. He heard a muffled curse, but didn't wait around for more.

Suddenly, Clint remembered some of the warnings he'd gotten about this particular stretch of land. Namely, he was reminded of the warnings regarding hunters' traps and such scattered in between the trees and buried in shallow patches of damp ground.

Unfortunately, the thing that had set those recollections into motion was the feel of rope tightening around his ankle and his leg being pulled out from underneath the rest of him.

Clint wasn't able to keep the surprised grunt from escaping his mouth as he felt his body lurch to one side and the rope tighten around his ankle. He'd run straight into a snare and was now in the process of being hauled up into one of the nearby trees like a prize catch. Of course, with all the natural camouflage, there was no way for him to have seen the rope or the trip wire that had sprung it without giving the men chasing him a good chance to catch up.

As he fell onto his back and was pulled over the soil, Clint swore he could feel the other men closing in on him. His stomach tightened and his teeth clenched together, but that could also have come from the fact that he was now starting to flip upside down while rising feet-first into the trees.

Clint righted himself as best he could so he could get a look at the predicament he was in. Lifting his other leg so that it was once again next to the one that had been snared, he felt the pain in his hips lessen just a bit. His limbs weren't flailing all akimbo, but he was still being hoisted into the air.

The rope around his ankle was thick as some of the older roots in the ground beneath him and felt every bit as strong. Rather than test the rope right away, Clint waited until he'd stopped rising through the air and started swinging back and forth at the end of the snare.

In a strange way, Clint's new position gave him the best perspective he'd had since he'd started running through the thick snarl of trees. Once he'd become accustomed to being upside down and swaying in the breeze, Clint took quick stock of his situation.

His hat had dropped from his head and was lying on the ground, but the modified Colt was still gripped in his hand. Those were the only bits of information Clint could gather before the men who'd been chasing him burst into view. Luckily for him, that was more than what he'd needed.

"Where'd he go?" the first man asked. He was short and had dark skin that blended in well with the muddied clothes he wore.

The second man to enter the area was taller and had a mop of coal-black hair that was a bigger mess than the roots under his feet.

Both men gripped rifles in their hands and wore plenty more weapons around their waists. In response to the first one's question, the second man grunted and shook his head. At that moment, a third man burst into the small clearing. The gun he held was still smoking.

"Where is he?" the third one asked.

The second man's voice took on a flustered tone. "The hell if I know!"

Clint swung in the air, wondering if the other three men

even knew about the trap that had swept him off his feet. For the moment, he decided to keep quiet and see how things panned out below.

"Well he didn't get far," the third one said. "He just took a shot at me a few seconds ago!"

The biggest of the three had yet to say a word. Instead, he looked around like a dog tracking the source of a scent tickling its nose. He shifted on his feet and became still the instant he spotted the hat on the ground next to his left boot.

"What's the matter with you?" the first man asked as he saw the second one squat down to get a look at something on the ground.

The other two men saw Clint's hat at the same time. After a second of glancing nervously around while crouching expectantly, they all wound up with their backs to one another. As one, they heard the creaking of rope over their heads and lifted their eyes upward.

They spotted Clint right away. All three of them raised their guns to take a shot, but didn't get further than that before Clint's Colt spat a gout of smoky lead in their direction.

Six shots came in quick succession. Two of them came from Clint and picked off the first and third of the other gunmen. The third came as a finger twitched against the trigger when its owner was blasted through the chest. The fourth and fifth came from Clint and the third man almost simultaneously.

The bigger man was jerked back a step as a round drilled through his shoulder. He fired a shot of his own, but only managed to blast some of the branches next to Clint's head. Another round caught the bigger man at the top of his forehead, burrowing straight down before exploding out the back of his neck.

That left Clint with only one more shot in his gun and he already knew exactly where it would go. Letting out a strained breath, he curled up so he was almost folded in half. From there, he could look straight up to where his foot was roped to one of the upper branches.

Clint sighted down the Colt's barrel and squeezed his trigger. The gun bucked in his hand as it sent a bullet straight through the rope connecting him to the top of the tree.

For a moment, Clint felt like he was still hanging suspended in the air. Then he realized that he was falling, and when the wind started to rush past his ears, it was a split-second before his shoulders slammed against the ground.

If not for the thick layers of roots and leaves covering the earth, Clint might have snapped his neck. As it was, he was able to roll with the impact and right himself while only losing the air from his lungs in the process. Without focusing on the dull pain that accompanied every breath, Clint reloaded the Colt with fresh rounds from his belt.

He snapped the cylinder shut and resumed his course through the jungle. As he ran, Clint thought back fondly to when there had been nothing but boardwalk and familiar dirt under his boots. It seemed like ages since he'd last walked upon those California streets. . . .

TWO

A month ago, Clint Adams was nowhere near a jungle. The closest thing he knew to being strung up from a tree was the talk he heard in a saloon of a recent hanging that had taken place a few counties away. The town's name was Santa Jenegal and it was situated in a hot stretch of California not too far from the Pacific Ocean.

On a clear day, someone standing on the porch of Santa Jenegal's finest hotel could see all the way to Mexico. It wasn't exactly a clear day, but Clint was doing his best to see as far as he could while nursing the beer in his hand.

It was getting close to evening and Clint was in the spot he normally inhabited at that time of the day. He'd been in Santa Jenegal for twelve days. After arriving on a matter concerning a chore for an old friend, Clint had decided to stay on for a while to soak up the atmosphere.

The chore had been a simple matter of running some documents from West Texas into California. If the postal service were more reliable in those parts, Clint wouldn't have been bothered with the task at all. But both he and Eclipse had been getting restless after a much deserved break, so Clint rode the Darley Arabian stallion almost to the edge of the country.

So far, it had been more than worth the trip.

"Excuse me, Mister Adams," came a voice from behind where Clint was standing.

Clint didn't have to take his eyes off the horizon to know who was talking to him. Studying the deep reds and splashes of dark gold that were special to that particular shore, he replied, "Go ahead, Samuel."

The stout Mexican was almost twice Clint's age, but carried himself like the other man's junior. He, like plenty of others who'd made the pretty little town their home, plainly reaped the rewards of the good life. "You're due to give that interview down at the *Gazette*."

Although Clint's hand dug out the watch from his pocket, it was another few seconds before he peeled his eyes from the scenery to look at it. The sun was on its way down and the resulting show was something that took his breath away. Sunsets weren't the same in every spot. The combination of a good vantage point and a peaceful heart made them truly something to behold.

Reluctantly, Clint looked down at the watch face. "I suppose I am."

"I was told you would be in big trouble if you missed your appointment."

"Is that a fact?"

"It sure is, señor," Samuel told him. "I was given permission to drag you to the *Gazette* by your heels if I needed to."

That brought an easy smile to Clint's face. When he turned around, the vision of the rich colors splayed out over the sands was still in his head. At that time of day, he wasn't too disappointed no matter where he stood. The sunset was casting its glow over the entire state right about then.

"Well, I wouldn't want to force you into something like that," Clint said. "It's too nice of a night to get myself hurt like that."

"Wise choice, señor. Is our card game still on later to-night?"

"Of course."

"Good. Then don't take too long. I need to win back what you took from me last time."

"I'll do my best," Clint said after downing the rest of his beer. "Of course, the reporters down at the *Gazette* tend to be awfully tenacious."

Samuel rolled his eyes and patted Clint on the arm. "Oh, I'm sure you'll do your best to tear yourself away." The sarcasm was dripping from his voice like molasses. "Of course, if I had a reporter like that wanting to write my story, I'd want to talk all night long."

Clint followed the Mexican's gaze farther down the boardwalk to a petite brunette making her way toward them. Her dress was a light purple and hugged the gener-ous curves of her breasts as if it had been painted onto her.

"All night," Samuel added, "and maybe some more the next morning."

Clint wasn't about to take his eyes off of the brunette now that he'd found something to watch that was prettier than the sunset. "Go on, Samuel," Clint said. "Let me have a word with this reporter."

Samuel retreated into the saloon across the street, shak-ing his head in wonder at the luck that seemed to bless some men.

The reporter in question made her way to where Clint was standing and stood with her hands on her hips. She eyed him without trying to hide the hunger in her eyes. "I was beginning to wonder if you were ducking me, Adams."

"Me? Ducking you?" Clint asked as he sidled up so that he was close enough to feel the heat coming off of her body. "Why would I ever want to do that?"

"Because you don't want your words turned on their ear to wind up in a yellowback novel."

"That thought has crossed my mind. After all, it wouldn't be the first time that's happened to me."

"Then you'd be insulting my integrity as a reporter."

Clint paused with his hand resting lightly on her shoulder. This same dance had been going on from the moment he'd ridden into town. Lyssa Olam practically met him on the outskirts of Santa Jenegal with pencil and paper in hand. Ever since then, she'd been tracking him down and pestering him for some exclusive time for her to conduct an interview. Considering the fact that she was a beauty with rich brown eyes, smooth hair that brushed against the nape of her neck and a body that could inspire any sculptor, Lyssa wasn't the easiest person to ignore.

Clint wasn't about to try too hard to ignore her, either. Although she had her moments, Lyssa had spent more time just being near him than trying to get any sordid details about his life. What had started as a professional meeting had quickly turned into something personal. It got more and more personal every night they spent together.

Moving in closer, Clint slipped one arm around Lyssa's back and used the other to smooth back a stray bit of shoulder-length hair that danced in front of her eyes. "I'd never insult your integrity, Miss Olam."

Lyssa waited until Clint's mouth was almost close enough to taste. Only then did she pull her head back a little and whisper, "If you think you can distract me one more time, you're wrong. You're even more wrong if you think I have any intention of letting slip my chance to interview the Gunsmith himself."

"You've had plenty of chances to ask me questions," Clint replied without being rattled by the sternness in her voice. "Usually, you just wind up breathing my name in the dark."

Lyssa was undeniably cute when she was flustered and this was one of those times. She wasn't exactly offended by what Clint had said, but she was definitely taken by surprise. Closing her eyes to try and collect herself, she felt Clint's embrace tightening around her.

Suddenly, her eyes snapped open and she said, "No. Not again. You promised me an interview. For God's sake, Clint, the last exciting thing to happen to this town was the opening of the two storefronts they call Chinatown."

"You want your story?" Clint asked. "Then you can get it. Ask your questions whenever you like."

"Really?" Lyssa turned her back to him so she could position her pencil over the paper she was holding. "First of all, how many gun battles do you think you've—"

She became distracted by the touch of Clint's lips against the back of her ear.

"Were you ever a real gunsmith? I mean—"

Clint's hands wrapped around her waist and held her while he began nibbling on her earlobe.

"What does it . . ." Lyssa let out a breath and turned so she could look him in the eyes. "Oh, hell," she whispered. "I guess the interview can wait."

THREE

Sometimes, when Clint and Lyssa got together, there was no telling where they would wind up. They might wake up in her bed or in the one he was renting. They might wind up sleeping under the stars in a camp not too far from town. This time, Clint's hotel was the closest place they could get to. With the heat running through both of their veins, neither one of them wanted to wait much longer before getting behind closed doors.

Clint's hands moved quickly up and down Lyssa's body. He traced the curves of her hips, continuing up along his firm round breasts. She knew the room just as well as he did and allowed herself to be eased backward until she felt her calves bump against the footboard of the bed.

Lyssa reached back and placed her palms against the bed, lowering herself down as Clint continued his gentle massage. After clearing the footboard, Lyssa fell back a little ways until her backside dropped onto the mattress. That left her legs dangling over the side, but that didn't cause her to skip a beat.

Clint leaned forward without taking his hands from her body. Lyssa's dress was askew and her skirts were bunched up close to her waist. That gave him a perfect view of her trim little body, which rivaled the show he'd been admiring in the sky before she'd shown up.

Lyssa's legs may have been short, but they were shapely and strong as they began to wrap around him. She reached up for Clint with one hand while pulling on the string that kept the front of her blouse shut over her breasts. Already, her nipples were hard and pressing against the thin cotton.

Feeling his own body reacting to the sight of her, Clint slid his hands up over her legs until he was reaching beneath her tussled skirts. Lyssa was wearing stockings held up by a garter belt. The feel of the silk and lace was more than enough to send another shiver down Clint's spine. That shiver only grew when his hand found the soft fabric of her panties, which were already hot and damp to the touch.

Clint's fingers traced over the delicate material, knowing full well what was waiting for him underneath. He could feel the gentle lines of her pussy and when he began stroking her, Lyssa responded with a long, shuddering breath.

"Oh God, Clint," she whispered as she closed her eyes and leaned her head back to savor what she was feeling. "You know just how to touch me."

As Clint worked his hand between Lyssa's thighs, he felt her legs ease open wider for him. He waited until the last possible second before peeling her panties to one side so he could move his fingers against the bare skin of her vagina.

Lyssa let out a moan that filled the room. Her body began to shake and she made little fists around the sections of the blanket she'd grabbed. Before too long, her eyes shot open and fixed upon Clint hungrily. Lyssa practically lunged forward to take hold of his shirt just so she could rip it off of him.

Not one to refuse a lady, Clint moved just right until his shirt came off. His pants were Lyssa's next target and she got those off in no time at all. Her hands reached out to cup him and stroke his thick, erect penis. Soon, both of her hands were massaging the small of his back and she was leaning forward with her mouth and eyes wide open.

Lyssa's lips were soft and pink as rose petals. Her tongue slid along the bottom of his cock as she began sucking on him. Her head bobbed back and forth as she worked him in and out. The next thing Clint felt was her hands pressing against his chest, forcing him back a few steps so she could climb off the bed and kneel in front of him.

As she continued to suck on his cock, Lyssa made a contented purring sound at the back of her throat. The feel of that sound almost made Clint's knees buckle. Not only did Lyssa notice that, but she found it amusing enough to settle on just the right spot to see if she could drive him even further out of his mind.

She succeeded.

Clint pulled in a deep breath as Lyssa worked her mouth and tongue on him. Just as he was starting to feel his climax rushing in on him, Clint eased away from her and did his best to calm down a bit.

"What's the matter?" Lyssa asked with a devilish smirk. "Did I do something wrong?"

Rather than answer that ridiculous question, Clint helped her to her feet and then promptly swept her off of them. He picked her up with both hands, causing Lyssa to hop into his arms and wrap her legs around him. Clint moved her to the side of the bed, dropped her onto it and pulled off the rest of her clothes.

Lyssa watched him with growing excitement. She kept her eyes on him the whole time, only moving when it was necessary for him to get her out of another layer of skirts or undergarments. Finally, she was naked on the bed in front of him.

Clint took a moment to drink in the sight of her. He could see Lyssa enjoyed having his eyes on her because she stretched out on the mattress as he quickly got undressed. From there, Clint lowered himself to the floor and pulled her to the edge of the mattress.

Lyssa's smooth, shapely legs draped over his shoulders. When Clint leaned in to start kissing the inside of her thighs, he felt her fingers slip through his hair. He worked his way in closer to the thatch of hair between her legs and when his tongue found the soft lips there, Clint heard her let out a long, trembling gasp.

Flicking his tongue out here and there, Clint tasted the smooth skin between Lyssa's legs. Her body was pressing against him and soon she was bucking against his face as an orgasm pulsed through her entire body. When she was able to collect herself a bit, she found Clint climbing onto the bed and settling down on top of her.

Her breaths were still coming in short gasps. Clint could feel her heart pounding as he lay on top of her and positioned himself between her legs. A few simple shifts was all it took for his erection to find her wet pussy and when he pushed his hips forward, Lyssa's back arched against the bed.

"Oh, Clint, yes," she breathed.

Clint moved his hands up along the sides of her naked body, along her outstretched arms and then finally closed them around her hands. He tightened his grip as his thrusts became more and more powerful, all but pinning her to the bed as he pumped in and out of her.

Lyssa opened her eyes and stared straight at him. There was no longer mischief or humor in her gaze. Her passion had completely overtaken him and the only thing she felt was desire and a hunger that only he could satisfy.

After letting her hands go, Clint straightened up so he was kneeling on the bed. He then took hold of her hips and lifted her slightly off the bed so he could resume his powerful rhythm. Lyssa was starting to tremble once more and without Clint to hold on to, she grabbed hold of the closest things she could find. She gripped the pillow under her head as if her life depended on it and her hips started bucking against him with just as much intensity.

Finally, another wave of pleasure raced through her system. Watching her give in like that made Clint feel his own climax approach. This time, he gave in as well. One more thrust pushed them both over the edge.

After that, it took a few more quiet minutes before either one of them could catch their breath.

FOUR

It was well past suppertime once Clint and Lyssa pulled their clothes on. After lying in each other's arms for a while and enjoying the darkness, the quiet that had taken over the room was broken by a low growling sound.

"Was that you?" Lyssa asked.

Clint waited a few moments before he realized the question wasn't about to go away on its own. "What can I say? I'm hungry."

After giving Clint a playful smack on the shoulder, Lyssa sat up so her back was resting against the headboard. "Come to think of it, I've worked up an appetite myself."

"Too bad most of the kitchens around here are closed for the night."

"Won't the hotel owners fix you anything?"

"I don't think some sandwiches and leftover dinner rolls will cut it."

"How about a nice, fat steak?"

The growling sound returned, only this time it was twice as loud. "That was just plain mean," Clint said as he clenched his stomach. "That is, unless you can deliver."

Lyssa looked over to him and winked. She was sitting up without doing a thing to cover her naked body. The moonlight was spilling in through the half-open window, giving her skin a pale glow. The night air was just chilly enough to make her nipples perk up a bit.

"I think I might just be able to do that," she said.

Now it was Clint's turn to perk up. "Really? I didn't think you liked to cook."

"I can cook, just so long as you don't mind scraping half of whatever it is off into the trash because it's too burnt to eat. Actually, I was thinking more along the lines of this place I know that caters to the occasional late request."

"A saloon?"

"No. Actually, it's the restaurant across from the *Gazette*. Plenty of times, we're up late working on the morning edition and we all get real hungry. We pay a little extra, but the cook finds it profitable enough to fill any requests with a smile on his face."

"Are the steaks any good?" Clint asked.

"Expensive, but yeah."

He was already pulling his clothes on and looking for his boots. "Right about now, I'd pay my weight in gold for a steak. Let's get moving."

To eyes that didn't know any better, Mike's Griddle was closed. The little storefront was right where Lyssa had promised, directly across from the narrow building that produced the *Jenegal Gazette*. Although he'd been in town for a while and had walked down that street plenty of times, Clint had overlooked Mike's Griddle completely.

Even if the place had shown any signs of life, the restaurant was small enough to be mistaken for part of the saddle shop next door to it. When they'd walked up to the front door, Clint doubted that anyone would be around to cook anything. That just made his stomach growl even louder.

"Trust me," Lyssa said as if she could read Clint's mind. "We'll be eating like kings before you know it."

She rapped on the door loudly enough to rattle it against its hinges. When nobody replied, she pounded her fist against the frame.

"You had to mention a steak," Clint groaned. "Now that's all I can think about."

She waved him off before leaning over to get a look through the rectangular window next to the door. The curtains were pulled to one side just enough for both of them to see the empty darkness inside the restaurant.

Just when it seemed that there was no more hope, Lyssa smacked her knuckles against the window so hard and so persistently that Clint thought she might just punch through the glass. At the moment he was about to hold her back from doing just that, Clint saw something stirring on the other side of the window.

First, there was just a rustle of one shadow against the other. Then, a slim trace of light could be seen. Finally, the outline of another door opening inside the place was illuminated by the vague flicker of a weak lantern.

Lyssa spotted all of this as well and stopped her assault on the front window. "There," she said with a proud smile. "I told you I could deliver."

"You almost delivered a broken window," Clint pointed out. "Now, let's just see if you're going to deliver one angry cook, to boot."

"He won't be angry. Mike just sleeps in the back and it takes a little work to wake him up again."

While they'd been talking, the lantern inside the restaurant had bobbed through the inner doorway and was working its way through the restaurant. Judging by the jerky motion of the light, the person holding it was either drunk or tripping on every piece of furniture along the way.

It wasn't until the light was inches from the glass that Clint was able to get a look at the face of the man holding the lantern.

"What the hell do you want?" the man inside the place asked.

Judging by the expression she wore, Lyssa might have just run into a neighbor while out for a stroll. "Hello, Mike," she said cheerily at the window. "Think you could toss some steaks on for me and my friend here?"

Mike appeared to be in his early forties. It also seemed as though he was afraid of razors and clean water because neither one of those things had come anywhere near him in a good week or three. His mouth hung open enough for Clint and Lyssa to get a look at his crooked teeth. Just when it seemed that he was going to snarl at them, Mike nodded and smiled.

"That you, Miss Olam?" he asked in a scratchy voice.

"Sure is. I know it's late, but—"

The rest of her explanation was cut short when the door was unlocked and pulled open by the scruffy man with the lantern.

"Come on in," Mike said. "Have a seat and I'll get some light in here. Be sure to lock the door behind you. Now, it's steaks you're after?"

"Sure is. We're working late and missed dinner."

Mike squinted toward Clint. "I didn't know he worked for the *Gazette*."

"Oh, he doesn't," Lyssa said with a dismissive wave aimed at Clint. "I'm interviewing him."

That seemed to be plenty explanation for Mike, since he'd already shifted his bleary eyes back toward Lyssa. "Steaks at this hour are gonna be a little steep," he said, clearly testing the waters.

"Price is no object," she assured the cook. "Just send the bill to Mister Adams, here."

Clint started to shoot a glare over to Lyssa, but she was already settled contentedly into her chair. It was also too late to say anything to Mike, because he was already done lighting a few more lanterns and was rushing back to the kitchen.

The moment he got his first whiff of those steaks, however, Clint wasn't even able to pretend he was annoyed with getting stuck with what promised to be a healthy bill.

FIVE

Lyssa hadn't been lying on either count. First of all, the steak that Mike prepared for him cost well more than double the normal price for a dinner. Second, it was worth every last penny.

Leaning back in his chair, Clint was taking a few breaths to clear some room for the last few bites that were on his plate. Although Mike wasn't shy about making them pay for waking him up, he also wasn't shy in heaping on all the extras he could find.

There were still enough potatoes, green beans and bread on Clint's plate to make another meal by themselves. The lanterns barely gave off enough light for them to see the inside of the restaurant, which made it easy to feel as if the rest of the world had simply stepped back and let them have this night for themselves.

"I never wanted to be a reporter," Clint said. "Until now, that is. Do all of you eat this well?"

"Not all the time, but Mike takes care of us. He stopped complaining once he realized the prices he could get away with charging us."

"You mean charging me."

Lyssa gave him a smirk. Although she was still in the

same seat she'd used when eating, she'd scooted closer to one of the lanterns fixed to the wall nearby. Apparently, one of the other reporters from across the street had been there earlier and left his copy of the *Jenegal Gazette* behind. She was now flipping through the folded pages and scanning every word carefully.

"I'll put the meal on my account so long as you give me that interview," she said.

Clint made a show of weighing the two options in his mind before finally shaking his head. "I think I'll just pay for the meal. That'll be less heartache for me."

"Do you honestly think I would make you look bad?"

"No, but I already get my name tossed around too often as it is. Adding more ink to that just puts more ideas in the heads of cowboys who are too drunk and too young to realize that taking me on to impress a saloon girl might just get them killed."

"Then I'll write a bad story," she offered.

"Yeah. That'll just make the rest of the gunfighters out there see me as easy pickings and come after me the moment I ride into town."

She ruffled the paper in front of her and shook her head. "That sounds awfully arrogant to me. You think the whole world is out to take a shot at you?"

"No, but the ones who are can make life into one hell of a trial."

Lyssa bent one finger, which caused a corner of the newspaper to fold down. Studying him with both eyes, she asked, "Do gunfighters really come after you like that?"

"Sometimes," Clint replied while scooping up the last bit of mashed potatoes from his plate.

"They want to make a name for themselves?"

"That, or they might want to look me up for something they think I've done to one of their friends or partners or brothers or Lord only knows who else."

"Could they be right?"

Clint paused and shrugged. "Certainly. Every man I've gone up against has friends, brothers, partners, or any combination of the three. But they also get the wrong idea. You know why?"

Letting out a heavy sigh, Lyssa covered her face with the newspaper. From behind her ink-stained screen, she recited, "Because rumors get spread around and made worse by reporters like me who fan the flames just to sell more papers."

"Exactly," Clint said while spearing the last few beans with his fork.

"You ever think a good reporter might just set the record straight with a good interview?" Lyssa asked.

"Yeah," Clint said, with only a momentary glance up from his plate. "That thought's crossed my mind."

A smile worked its way onto Lyssa's face. Once she saw that Clint had already looked back to his plate without saying that she was the talented reporter he was referring to, she grumbled and snapped the newspaper in her hand.

Clint waited another few seconds before letting her off the hook. Actually, that was as long as he could keep himself from laughing at the way Lyssa squirmed in her seat. "I'm just teasing," he said.

"Oh, no," Lyssa sneered. "You made your bed and now you sleep in it, Clint Adams. I wouldn't help you if your life depended on it."

Clint pushed away from the table and tossed his napkin onto his plate. He walked over to Lyssa and sat down in a chair right beside her. "I don't know about you, but sleeping in my bed wasn't exactly what I had in mind."

Although he couldn't see it, Clint could feel the mischievous smile coming back to Lyssa's face. Her hands kept the newspaper held high in front of her, however.

"Too late to get on my good side," Lyssa said from behind the *Gazette*. "That ship has already sailed."

Clint scooted his chair so that he would be looking directly into Lyssa's face if the newspaper weren't between them. After a few moments, he tapped gently upon the tightly gripped paper. "I'll answer any question if you ask it right now."

The newspaper wavered slightly as Lyssa shook her head behind it. "I'm not falling for that. Not again."

"Come on. I mean it this time."

"Nope."

Behind the paper, Lyssa was doing her best to keep the sound of amusement from her voice. Despite the fact that Clint stubbornly refused to sit down for an interview, she'd been piecing bits together here and there. It was at times like these that she got the best pieces. And the longer she kept him talking, the fuller her story would become.

Every now and then, she could see a welt the size of a man's fingertip come and go in the newspaper. Clint tapped insistently while he started gently rubbing her knee. It was a dance that they'd been doing since Clint had gotten to town and neither one of them seemed to be getting tired of it just yet.

Lyssa could feel her resolve breaking down. Whether or not she got her story became less of an issue. Dancing with Clint, on the other hand, was enough fun to justify possibly missing out on the story she was after.

In her mind, she counted off the moments that she was going to make him stew for what he'd said. Just when she was about to make him think he'd broken her down, Lyssa realized something odd.

The tapping had stopped.

Clint wasn't saying anything.

He wasn't even rubbing her knee.

After a few more moments of silence, Lyssa started to wonder if she was alone in the restaurant.

"Clint?" she asked while lowering the paper. "What's the mat—"

Clint's hand snapped out to grab the top of the paper.

"Hold it," he said while keeping the newspaper where it had been previously. "Let me read this."

"What? Are you kidding me? You want to read? Now?!"

Since she couldn't get the paper out of Clint's hands, Lyssa let it go so she could stand up and walk around it herself. She found Clint leaning forward in his chair with the *Gazette* dangling from his hand. He was studying every word of a column written on the third page.

"If this is a joke, it's not funny," Lyssa warned.

Clint shook his head. "This isn't a joke." He then tapped the top of the story he was reading. "I know this man."

Now, Lyssa studied the newspaper in Clint's hand. At the top of the story, in bold print, was written:

RENOWNED BOUNTY HUNTER DANIEL MILLER
PRESUMED MISSING IN AMAZONIAN JUNGLE

SIX

Clint knew well enough that newspapers took plenty of liberties with how they presented their news. While some publications were more trustworthy than others, they were all out to sell papers. For this reason, Clint knew that the story he was looking at might not be as bad as it seemed.

For instance, the word "renowned" had been used to describe Danny Miller. Clint knew Danny Miller fairly well and although the man was a bounty hunter, he was a long ways from being renowned. He'd pulled in a few known men and gotten into some scrapes, but "renowned" was pushing it just a bit.

On the other hand, there weren't too many different interpretations for the phrase "presumed missing." That one was pretty bad no matter how Clint tried to look at it. Fortunately, he had a source of his own to consult.

"Do you know the man who wrote this?" Clint asked as he held the paper so Lyssa could get a better look at the story.

She looked it over quickly and nodded. "That's one of Mark's pieces. I work with him every day."

"Does he know what he's doing?"

"None of us care too much for lying in print," she said

in a scolding tone. "That does tend to hamper a reporter's reputation."

"Some aren't worried about their reputations," Clint replied as he brought the paper around so he could see the story once more. "Believe me, I know all about that."

The expression on Lyssa's face softened quite a bit. "I know. I've read some of the garbage that's been printed about you. At least, I'm pretty sure it's garbage."

Clint shook his head at the way Lyssa kept on trying to get something out of him no matter what else was going on. "I'd say there's a better than average chance that most of what's in print about me is complete fiction. Half of the rest might have something to it. What I need to know about is the man who wrote this."

"Mark's a fine reporter. Not as good as me, but he pulls his weight."

"Do you know anything about this story?"

"I heard him talking about something to do with the Amazon and the jungle, but I didn't pay too much attention to it," she replied. "I've barely got enough time to write my own stories."

"Do you know where I can find him?"

Already, Lyssa was moving up next to Clint and nibbling on his ear. "He'll be at the *Gazette* tomorrow morning, just like I will. We've got some time to kill until then."

But Clint pushed back from her and dropped enough money onto the table to cover the inflated cost of the meal. From there, he immediately started walking toward the door. "I can't wait until morning. I need to talk to him now."

"Now?"

"Right now."

Lyssa let out an aggravated breath and began reaching out to run her hand over Clint's chest. Recent memories flooded her mind, but stopped once she got a look at the crumpled paper that had put the burr under Clint's saddle.

"Do you really know this Miller person?" she asked.

"I'm pretty sure I do. That's why I need to talk to the reporter who wrote this."

"And what happens if this is the man you know?"

"I'm not sure. First I need to make certain that this information is accurate. If it is, I'll take it from there."

Lyssa followed Clint in a huff. "Of course it's accurate. The *Gazette* isn't some rag that's published to spread rumors and gossip."

Clint's hand was resting on the door frame. He moved it down to keep Lyssa from getting past him. "If you can vouch for every word in your newspaper being 100 percent accurate, then I'll be satisfied. And if you can tell me that nothing gets blown out of proportion to make a story better or boost your sales, then that's all I need to hear."

There was plenty that Lyssa wanted to say. That much was obvious just by looking at the way she clenched her jaw and glared back at Clint. But, rather than say anything, she let out a sigh and smacked Clint on the arm.

"Come on," she grumbled. "Let's go talk to Mark."

Clint fought back the urge to smirk. At least, he was able to hold it back long enough for Lyssa to huff past him and out of the restaurant.

SEVEN

Mark was a tall fellow with closely cropped hair. His eyes had dark circles under them, but were relatively clear, considering the late hour. He'd answered the door after Lyssa had knocked on it a few times with an impatient flurry of knuckles. The door to the small house creaked open to reveal the reporter still in a rumpled suit.

"Yeah?" the man grumbled. "What is it?" When he blinked a few times and let his eyes adjust to the darkness, Mark was able to see who was standing at his door. "Lyssa? Is that you?"

"It's me, all right. Mind if I come in?"

Mark began hurriedly to straighten his suit as his face glowed with the welcome surprise. "Sure, sure. Come on in. I just got in myself."

"By the way," Lyssa said with an off-handed wave, "this is Clint Adams. Clint, this is Mark Albertson."

The disappointment at realizing that Lyssa wasn't alone was like a fog that clouded over Mark's face. Clint almost felt bad for the other man as he walked into the fellow's house before Mark could close the door on him. Apparently, Lyssa wasn't exactly unappreciated among her co-workers.

29

"Hello, Mark," Clint said. "Sorry to bust in on you like this."

"Oh, uhh, it's no problem," Mark said in a valiant effort to cover the plans he'd had for himself and Lyssa, which had been destroyed almost instantly. "What can I do for you?"

"You remember that story you wrote about the bounty hunter lost in the jungle?" Lyssa asked.

If Mark had been disappointed before, his spirits were lifted the moment he heard mention of that story. "Of course I remember it! I was just reading it over dinner. I think it came out really—"

"Clint wants to ask you some questions about it."

Although a little put off by the interruption, Mark was still eager to talk. That eagerness lasted even after he'd shifted his eyes to Clint. "You read my story?"

"Not all of it," Clint replied. "But it's important that I go straight to the source where that's concerned."

"Certainly."

"Clint wants to know if you made any embellishments," Lyssa cut in. The last word in her sentence reeked of accusation and wasn't lost on the other reporter.

Still rumpled in appearance, Mark straightened up and lifted his chin as if he were about to speak to the president himself. "I am an honest journalist, Mister Adams, and I take my job very seriously."

"Good, then maybe you can tell me where you got your information regarding Danny Miller."

For a moment, Mark continued to look at Clint with indignation. Then his expression changed a bit as he got his mind around the request Clint had just made. "I can't reveal my source."

"This isn't something about some secret government plan or something like that," Clint said. "This is just about a man who's turned up missing. That man is no stranger to me and if he's in trouble, I'd like to help him."

Clint could tell the reporter was softening a bit around the edges. Mark's eyes were still darting between Clint and Lyssa, but he no longer seemed as defensive as he had a moment earlier.

"Why else would you write that story?" Clint asked. "Unless you wanted to do some good."

There were plenty of other reasons to write that story and Clint was well aware of most of them. Apart from simply meeting a deadline and filling space in a morning edition, there was the possibility of earning a promotion or any number of rewards that reporters strove for. But the tone in Clint's voice made it seem that he could only comprehend the purest motive for Mark's action. He hoped that would appeal to the essence inside almost every reporter's soul.

"I saw your story and it hit a nerve," Clint said, hoping to touch on the nerve that was inside every writer. "It caught my attention and it could do some good. It might even save a man's life."

"What do you want from me?" Mark asked.

"First off, I need to know if that story is true."

Once again, Mark bowed up. "Of course it is. I told you before."

"In that case, you know damn well that Danny Miller is in trouble. How did you even find out that he was missing?"

"Didn't you read my story?"

"Yes, but I need to hear it from you," Clint insisted. "And I need to know whatever you might have left out of the story."

After a few silent moments, Mark nodded and stepped back farther into his home. He waved them in as if that motion were taking up almost all the energy he had. "Come on in, then. And shut the door behind you."

Lyssa seemed to know her way well enough and was already stepping into the sitting room where Mark was headed. She dropped herself down onto one of a few creaking chairs and waited for the other two to catch up.

Clint found his way into the room, which didn't have much else inside it besides the chairs, a table and a battered footstool. What made the room seem much fuller than it was were the shelves that lined every wall. Each shelf was made from thick lumber and was sagging in the middle due to the weight of all the books on it.

Mark found himself a chair closest to the door, which left Clint with a choice between one chair that was in the middle of the room and another that looked like it would fall apart under a heavy glare.

Clint pulled the chair from the middle of the room so he could sit with his back to one of the bookshelves. Leaning forward, he fixed his eyes upon the weary reporter.

"Go on, Mark," Clint said, doing his best to keep the urgency from his voice. "Let's hear it."

EIGHT

"I heard about Danny Miller a few times over the years," Mark explained. "He never was quite like all the other bounty hunters I've met. Most of those men are killers, plain and simple. The only thing that separates them from the animals they track down is where they get their money from."

So far, Clint couldn't disagree with the reporter. Even if he did find fault with what Mark was saying, Clint wasn't about to interrupt the man now that he was moving along at a good pace.

Keeping his eyes focused upon the floor at his feet, Mark went on to say, "Danny was always full of good stories. I decided to print one of them, since I was actually able to back it up with some fact."

"How much fact are we talking about here?" Clint asked.

Just when it seemed that the reporter was going to put up his guard one more time, he shrugged and let it down. "Actually, I verified the name of the man Danny claimed to have brought in and that the outlaw was indeed hung when Danny said he was. Since the rest of the story didn't seem too far out of line, I wrote it up and it was published. Sold a lot of papers, too."

"I'll bet it did. Danny always did have a flair for story-telling."

"Yeah, well it might not all have been totally true," Mark admitted. "But it was harmless enough and made for a good read."

Lyssa let out a cross between a huff and a sigh. She'd pulled her head back and was looking at Mark with utter surprise. That expression didn't last long once Clint fixed his eyes upon her. The moment she turned away, she all but admitted to doing the same thing Mark had admitted to himself.

"Anyway," Mark continued, "I wasn't exactly proud of it, so I never really spoke to Danny much again. He kept hounding me with more stories and more promises of bringing some real dirt into the light. But what he told me just kept getting more and more outrageous."

"But you still published some of it, didn't you?" Clint asked.

Since there wasn't any real judgment in Clint's tone, Mark nodded. "Every now and then, yeah. And most of the times, I kept it simple. Until one time when I met up with him in Sacramento.

"It was during a conference that I was covering for the *Gazette*. Danny found me and said that it was fate that we should meet up like that just then. He was all worked up about something and I just figured it was another one of his stories."

"What was it?" Clint prodded.

"It was a story, all right. A hell of a big one. It was so big that I thought he had to be drunk the minute he told me. When he said he wasn't, I turned my back on him and vowed not to print another word that came from his mouth." Looking over to Lyssa, Mark added, "I mean, enough's enough, right?"

Lyssa nodded.

"What did he tell you?" Clint asked. His patience was wearing thin and it was getting more and more difficult to keep that from being too obvious.

Shaking his head, Mark ran his fingers over his scalp while letting out a measured breath. "Danny told me that he was on the trail of a man and that, once he caught up to him, that man would make him rich enough to retire for good."

"That sounds like what he said about most of his bounties," Clint said.

"Sure, but this wasn't about collecting any bounty. It was about something going on down south. And by south, I don't mean Mexico. Danny started talking about heading into Peru and cutting through the jungle to get to this other man. Then he started going on about the treasure. That's when I started to think he'd been drinking too much."

Hearing that caused Lyssa to snap forward as though she'd been pulled by a rope tied around her neck. "Treasure? What treasure?"

Although Clint wasn't as easy to read, he was still plenty interested. He'd moved a bit closer to the edge of his seat and narrowed his eyes into slits. Through those slits, he stared straight into Mark's eyes and took a good long look at what was going on in there. "Yeah," he said. "What treasure?"

NINE

Mark nodded to Lyssa before meeting Clint's stare. "He told me about some treasure down in the jungle. There was supposed to be some jewels and such, but most of it was gold. Incan gold, as a matter of fact."

Clint had stared down plenty of men. In fact, his livelihood had depended on that very skill when the stakes in a poker game were high enough. Throughout all the years of sitting at those high-stakes games, Clint had become a good judge of character.

Although it was hard to say whether or not Danny Miller had been drunk at the time or not, it was apparent that Mark Albertson believed every word he was saying. Clint would have staked his life on it.

"How much gold?" Lyssa asked excitedly.

"Enough to make him a king," Mark replied. "At least, that's what Danny said. There was supposed to be some village or temple or something hidden in the jungle."

"Your story said it was a temple," Clint said.

Mark shrugged while lowering his eyes. "That is what I wrote, but I don't think even Danny was too sure about it. If he was, he didn't make it clear to me."

Strangely enough, hearing that admission made Clint believe the rest of what Mark had said even more.

"Danny told me he found out about this when he was on a job, tracking some mercenary over the border into Mexico," Mark continued. "Apparently, Danny wasn't the only one after this fellow and things got pretty ugly."

"Yeah," Clint said as he thought back to the last few times he and Danny had crossed paths. "Things tended to go that way around him."

"It sounded a lot like the other stores Danny told me. There was plenty of shooting and such, but it wound up with this mercenary getting away and nearly killing Danny in the process. The chase went on and Danny followed him all the way into some little border town."

"Do you remember the name of that town?" Clint asked. "It wasn't in the paper."

"No, it wasn't." Mark nodded at Clint and gave him a warm smile. "You really did read the story."

"If this turns out all right, I'll even write a letter to the editor."

Mark chuckled at that and pressed his fingertips to his eyebrows as he took a moment to think. Before too long, his head snapped up and his eyes took on an excited glimmer. "Perro Poco! That was the name of the place. It was a town called Perro Poco."

"Do you know what side of the border it's on?"

After another intense thinking session, Mark shook his head. "Not for certain. Does it matter?"

"You'd be surprised how much that could matter," Clint said. "What happened after that?"

"Well, Danny told me about the treasure, saying he heard about it when he was following this mercenary. Turns out the mercenary is setting himself up as some kind of ruler down in that jungle and doesn't much care about spilling blood on his way to getting at that gold."

Leaning forward, Mark added, "Here's the interesting part. Danny said that he knew something the others didn't. He even thought he was ahead of everyone else looking for that gold."

"What was it?" Lyssa asked.

Mark leaned back again until his shoulders bumped against the back of the chair. He held his hands out, open and palms up. "I don't know. He said he'd tell me all about it when he got back. I didn't hear anything about him after that. I was supposed to meet him a few weeks later and he would tell me the rest of the story. He never showed up."

"So, you think he's missing?" Clint asked.

"I know he's missing," Mark said without the slightest hint of uncertainty. "He never missed out on a chance of getting into the newspaper. Not ever."

Clint nodded. He knew enough about Danny Miller to vouch for Mark's last statement.

"But it wasn't just that," Mark added. "Danny contacted me through the mail all the time. You know, to set up meetings and such so he could tell me about what he'd been doing. I got a letter from him that said he was in trouble and that if he didn't come back by the fourteenth that he would probably never make it out of that jungle."

"The fourteenth was only a few days ago," Clint said.

"No. It was the fourteenth of last month."

"Do you still have that final letter?" Clint asked.

"Let me take a look."

As Mark rummaged through stack upon stack of papers, Clint did his best to keep his patience. All the while, he felt like he was being strung along for the purpose of building up to a good ending, when all he wanted was a straight account of what had happened. By the look on face, Lyssa seemed to be enjoying every minute of it.

"Here it is," Mark said when he finally walked back to his seat. He handed over a piece of paper that was folded neatly into thirds.

Clint took the paper and opened it. The only thing written there that Mark hadn't already mentioned was a name. "Who's Graham Farnsworth?" Clint asked.

Mark shrugged. "Hell if I know."

All Clint had to do was turn in Lyssa's direction and he suddenly felt the letter get snatched from his hand. She skimmed over the words, hungrily committing every last one of them to memory.

"That's all I have for you, Mister Adams," Mark said. "I swear."

Clint gave the reporter another careful glance before nodding. "I believe you."

"I just hope it's enough. For what it's worth, Danny Miller seemed like a good enough sort. A little rambunctious, but his heart was in the right place."

"His heart, maybe," Clint said as he took the letter from Lyssa and handed it back to Mark. "But his head wasn't always in that same place."

Mark stood up, which prompted the other two to do the same. "I also think Danny's in serious trouble. That's why I wrote the story in the paper. Since nobody else seemed to want to listen, I thought I might be able to reach someone who did."

TEN

Clint was the one to open the front door, but Lyssa was the first one to step out through it. She exploded from Mark's house as though she'd been fired from a cannon. Her feet barely seemed to touch the ground as she raced outside and crossed the street.

"Did you hear that?" she asked.

Clint shut the door once he was through and followed her. "Yeah, I heard it. I was in there. The question is why you hadn't heard it before. Don't you work with him?"

"Sure I do, but we don't tell everyone what we're working on. If it's too good, it might get stolen right out from under us."

"Real honest bunch of reporters working over at the *Gazette*," Clint said sarcastically. "Fine bunch of integrity you all have got there."

"It's a tough job, Clint. You know that." In the blink of an eye, Lyssa had shaken off the effects of Clint's comment and was back to the excited state she'd been in moments ago. "I looked over that story when it was printed, but didn't think much of it. Mark writes up so much about shootings and bounty hunters that I thought this was just a load of nonsense. But this sounds like the genuine article."

"It might be."

"Might be?" Lyssa stopped and spun around quick enough to send her hair whipping around her face and neck. "*Might be?* I've got instincts, Clint, and they're all telling me this can be big. Maybe even bigger than what Mark thinks."

"I've got instincts, too," Clint replied. "And right now, they're telling me that this could just as easily be something serious or nothing whatsoever."

"How could it be nothing?" Lyssa asked, placing her hands on her hips.

"Danny could be drunk somewhere. He could be in jail after taking a swing at the wrong man in a saloon. He could have met a good woman and decided to settle down. Hell, he could have gotten wrapped up in a card game and missed his stage to wherever he was headed. It could be plenty of things other than him going missing. As a reporter, you should know that just as well as I do."

"And what if it isn't, Clint? What if none of those things happened and a man's in serious trouble?"

"Then I guess you've got yourself a story. Isn't that what you're after?"

Clint turned away from Lyssa and started walking down the street. He was headed in the direction of his hotel, but only made it a few paces before being stopped by a sudden obstruction in his path. That obstruction was a brunette with her arms folded sternly across her chest.

"That wasn't fair," Lyssa said.

"Wasn't it? Then why are you so anxious to hear about some bounty hunter who was just the source of some nonsense accounts before today?"

She thought about that for a moment and shrugged. "Not all of Mark's stories were nonsense. I'll admit that."

Clint stepped up so that he was toe to toe with her, knowing that she wouldn't take a step back. When she held her ground, Lyssa found herself looking directly into

Clint's eyes. He wasn't angry, but he was plainly not going to let her get away with anything, either.

"And what about the fire in your eyes at the mention of treasure?" Clint asked. "You looked like a kid who'd just dug up a pirate's chest in the middle of a field."

She shrugged again. This time wasn't even as convincing as the first. "It's not something I hear every day." Suddenly regaining her edge, Lyssa returned Clint's glare with interest. "What about you? Whether it was the treasure or Danny being missing, there was something in what Mark said that you believed. Tell me I'm wrong and I'll tell you that you're lying through your teeth."

Clint was tempted to put that to the test. Then again, he'd been around enough reporters to know that their skill at reading people could rival that of the best poker players.

"I know Danny well enough to believe that he could get himself into a mess like this," Clint said. "I also know that he tangles with plenty of men that could make him disappear for good."

Lyssa nodded and let her smile grow a bit more. "And if he's half the bounty hunter Mark says he is, this Danny Miller had to have pissed off some very bad men."

"I've never heard of this place, Perro Poco."

"It's only about a day's ride from here."

"You know where it is?"

She nodded again. "And I can get you there quicker than anyone else could. Probably twice as quickly as you could get there on your own."

Now it was Clint's turn to laugh. "Oh, no you don't. If you want to help, you can tell me the quickest way to get there, but you're not coming with me."

"Just try to stop me."

Clint stepped forward until he was practically standing on Lyssa's feet. He looked down at her until it seemed that he was a mountain getting set to bury the reporter. "I can stop you."

Reluctantly, Lyssa said, "I believe you, Clint." Her hands came up to rub against his stomach, working their way up until she was lightly massaging his chest. When she looked up again, her eyes were wide and inviting. "But I'd still like to go with you. I really would."

The tactics she was using were as plain as the sky over their heads. Even so, that didn't make them any less effective.

"If you do come with me, you need to do exactly what I tell you at the exact time I tell you to do it," Clint said sternly.

"Of course!"

Shaking his head, Clint continued walking to his hotel. "All right, then. I need to get my things. Pack what you need and nothing more. Meet me at the stables in twenty minutes. If you're late, I'm leaving without you."

Lyssa was already running down the street. "You won't regret this, Clint! I promise."

Part of Clint was already regretting it.

ELEVEN

Not only did Lyssa avoid being late meeting Clint at the stables, she actually beat him there. By the time he walked into the drafty building with his saddlebags slung over his shoulder, Clint spotted her climbing onto the back of her spotted mare.

Lyssa's horse was colored as if it had started off white and had been darkened slightly with a few coats of dust. A few clusters of brown spots were scattered on the animal's right shoulder and left hindquarter. Its mane was light tan in color, which almost matched the saddle strapped to its back.

Clint went through the motions of saddling his own black Darley Arabian. Eclipse was so used to the process that the stallion knew exactly when to shift or turn on his feet. In no time at all, Clint was tightening the last buckle and climbing into the well-worn saddle.

"You're a smart man, Clint," Lyssa said.

"And you're a stubborn woman."

"I need to be if I'm going to be a good reporter. Did you know that only half of my stories get published under my real name? The rest come out under a man's name so they'll be taken seriously."

Clint was already flicking his reins and getting Eclipse moving toward the stable doors. He'd just made it into the street before Lyssa was coming up alongside of him.

"If Danny really is in trouble, then it's best that it sees the light of day," she said.

"Especially if the story gets put out under your real name, right?"

"Yes. And once that story comes out, whoever did this to that poor man will be shown for the murderous dogs they are."

Clint let out a grunting laugh as he steered onto the street that would take them out of town. "Have you even met Danny Miller?"

"Well . . . no. But I'm sure he's a fine man."

"He's a bounty hunter, a gambler and a liar. You know why he became a bounty hunter?"

"No."

"Because he tracked down a group of horse thieves so he could divert attention from the three horses he'd stolen himself."

"Oh, well I'm sure there was a good reason for it."

"Sure," Clint said. "Just like there's a good reason for horse thieves to be strung up about a day after they're caught."

Although he wasn't looking at her, Clint could feel Lyssa's frustration building by the second.

"Well if he's such a scoundrel," she said, "then why are you going off to help him?"

"Because he's actually not as bad as he seems."

Lyssa's face brightened as she leaned back a bit in her saddle. "I knew it. A hard man struggling to better himself against impossible odds. That's the kind of story that gets onto the front page."

"Before you get too excited, you should know that he's still not the straightest arrow out there. I've wanted to kick Danny's ass plenty of times myself."

"But now you want to keep him alive," Lyssa pointed out.

"Now I do," Clint agreed. "But if this turns out to be some kind of hoax or some half-baked scheme of his, I'll keep him alive just so I can make him regret being born."

"You don't want him to get hurt," Lyssa said, as though she'd already seen enough of Clint's soul to know everything he was thinking. "Otherwise, you wouldn't be riding down to some little town in the middle of nowhere to check in on him."

"If it was more than a day's ride away, I probably would have passed."

"I don't think so. Everything I've ever heard about you tells me that you seldom pass over the opportunity to help someone if you can. That's what lands you in so many newspapers."

"Actually, what lands me in so many papers is reporters who can't stop sticking their noses into my affairs."

"Is that why you brought me along?" Lyssa asked. "So I can see how the Gunsmith truly is when push comes to shove?"

"I brought you along because I know you'd dog my trail even if I tied you to a tree. At least this way I can keep you in my sights."

Lyssa gave Clint a wicked smirk and said, "Tie me to a tree? That sounds fun." With that, she snapped her reins and got her mare running down the trail, which led into the wide open land south of town.

"We'll see about that," Clint said under his breath. "I brought along plenty of rope."

With Eclipse ready to run, all it took was a touch of the reins on his back to send the Darley Arabian bolting toward Perro Poco.

TWELVE

When Clint spotted Perro Poco for the first time, he was instantly grateful that he'd brought Lyssa along. If not for the reporter's instructions, it might have taken almost triple the amount of time to get there. In fact, the town was so small that Clint could very well have overlooked it altogether.

By the time they reached the little town, Clint swore that he'd ridden back and forth over the border at least five times. The trail had started winding around everything from rock outcroppings to overhangs to rivers that splashed around as though even the water didn't know where it was going. Several times along the way, Clint needed to stop to get his bearings.

It never really helped.

The first glimpse they'd caught of the town was a pair of shacks. They were in such a bad state of disrepair that leaning against one another seemed to be the only thing keeping them from falling over. When she'd spotted the shacks, Lyssa pointed to them proudly and declared, "There it is."

Clint brought Eclipse to a stop, stood up in the stirrups and took a look around. When his eyes found Lyssa once more, he said, "There what is?"

"The town," she insisted, poking her finger toward the shacks. "Perro Poco. There it is."

Giving the reporter a weary glance, Clint snapped the reins and started riding toward the shacks. Even Eclipse seemed reluctant to approach the buildings out of fear of accidentally knocking one over.

The shacks were each about twice as big as an outhouse and not even half as sturdy. Clint gave them a wide berth and continued riding down the trail, which took him over a rise and around a bend. The rise was just big enough to keep him from seeing what was directly ahead of him.

After cresting the rise, Clint stopped and took a look at the land in front of him. There were a few more shacks and they even seemed to be capable of standing on their own. Some people moved around those shacks and a cart even rode between them.

"You see?" Lyssa said as she rode up next to Clint. "Perro Poco. Just like I promised."

Clint pulled in a breath through his nose and winced. "At least I can see where they got the name for this place. It smells like a dog's backside."

"A little dog's backside," Lyssa corrected. "That is, unless my Spanish is worse than I thought."

"Right."

Since the stench hanging over the town wasn't going to lift anytime soon, Clint pulled in a deep breath and headed down over the rise. Lyssa was never more than a few feet from him and, judging by the excited look on her face, she'd just discovered some previously unknown promised land.

Perro Poco wasn't much more than a few weather-beaten buildings clustered around a fat spot in the road. A few less fortunate shacks were situated behind the rest, but half of those had already collapsed under their own weight. Plenty of the lumber used to make the buildings was blackened and scorched. Apparently, the town had been burnt down and built up at least once or twice.

Like most little dogs out on their own, this one had become as tough as it was mangy.

Clint rode Eclipse to the second building on the right side of the street. It was the only one with a hitching post in front of it and there were already two other tired mules standing there. He swung down from the saddle and motioned for Lyssa to do the same.

"I thought you'd want me to stay out here," Lyssa chided.

"You can if you want," Clint said as he shifted his eyes along both sides of the street. "But I wouldn't recommend it."

Lyssa followed Clint's gaze and saw that several sets of squinting eyes were already intently focused on them. Every one of those eyes was set deeply in a dirty face that regarded Lyssa as if she were a thick cut of steak on an otherwise empty plate.

Shifting her eyes away from the onlookers who had sprouted along the street, Lyssa all but jumped down from her saddle. "I see what you mean."

Clint waited until she was on her feet before stepping up to the door that led into the combination saloon and hotel. The only way for him to tell that much was the words scrawled onto either side of the door frame in what appeared to be charcoal.

One side of the frame said "SALLOON" and the other side read "HOTEL." He just hoped their hospitality was a little better than their spelling.

The inside of the place was exactly what Clint expected. A bar, constructed of a few long planks laid across some overturned crates, ran along one side. A row of doors ran along the other and two tables took up what little space remained. The only light came from the several cracks in the walls and roof that allowed sunlight to leak through.

Four men were in the place. Two of them sat at a table, one leaned against the bar and the fourth stood behind it. The man behind the bar was Mexican, but it was impossible to know that much about anyone else, since they kept their faces angled toward the floor.

"You want a drink," the barkeep said in a manner that was more of a statement than a question. When he spotted Lyssa, he flashed a filthy grin and added, "Or a room."

Clint walked up to the bar, making a point to meet any stare that came his way. He needed to look at every set of eyes in the room, but everyone apart from the bartender wasn't interested in looking back at him just yet.

"I just want to know about a man who passed through here a while ago," Clint said.

"Drink or room."

"Pardon me?"

"Drink or room," the barkeep said as if Clint's previous statement hadn't even been uttered. "You pick one or leave. I ain't here to talk."

Clint removed some money from his pocket and held it so the barkeep could see the folded bills. He was also careful to position himself so only the barkeep could see the money. Peeling off one dollar, Clint kept the rest in hand and said, "The lady and I will have a drink. If you answer a few questions, I sure would appreciate it."

The barkeep held out his hand and rubbed his fingers together as if he were trying to start a fire. Clint handed over the wad of money, which was enough to make the Mexican's eyes grow to the size of saucers.

"What man you looking for?" the barkeep asked.

"He's around my height, light brown hair, pale skin. Carries his weight in guns."

It wasn't until that last part that the Mexican started to nod. "Oh, yeah. I seen that man. It's been a while, though."

"How long?"

"A few weeks. Maybe a month. Could be longer, I don't really keep track of things like when gringos come and go."

"How long did he stay here?" Clint asked.

"One night. I remember that because I would have asked him to leave if he wanted to stay any longer. All them guns make my customers nervous."

All this time, Lyssa had been watching the other men in the saloon carefully. Every last one of them was carrying at least two firearms in plain sight. "Oh, I'm sure you cater to a real sensitive crowd." She grunted.

"You want to stay, *chiquita*?" the barkeep asked. "I can make you real comfortable. You make a real good living in Perro Poco."

"We'll think about it," Clint responded before Lyssa could open her mouth. Putting himself between her and the barkeep, he added, "First I need to take care of this business of mine. Where did this gringo with the guns go after he left here?"

The barkeep sank away from Clint's glare. After tightening his fist around the money he'd been given, he shrugged and said, "I don't follow him, but he did ask about something."

"What did he ask about?"

"I tell you if you buy some more drinks. I'm sure you got more in those pockets of yours, señor."

Clint let out a sigh. He'd seen this coming as if it had already happened. It was just a shame that some folks were so damn easy to predict.

"You know what else I've got in my pocket?" Clint asked. Before the barkeep could blink, Clint had flipped open his jacket to reveal the modified Colt holstered at his hip. "Now earn that money I already gave you before I take it out of your hide."

The barkeep glanced around at the other locals in the saloon. When he saw that the others couldn't turn away fast enough, he said, "Ernesto. Go talk to Ernesto across the street. That's where your gringo friend went."

"Thank you," Clint said as he straightened his jacket. "Thank you kindly."

THIRTEEN

Although the directions weren't the best, "across the street" only consisted of four other buildings for Clint and Lyssa to check. One of those was abandoned, which made the search that much easier. After knocking on the second door, Clint hit pay dirt.

"Hello there," Clint said amiably. "I'm looking for Ernesto."

"You got business here?" the scruffy old man on the other side of the door asked.

Since there was no sign posted that Clint could see, he checked the door frame for any words scrawled on the wood. He came up short there as well. "My business is with Ernesto. Is he here or not?"

"Why you want to see Ernesto?"

"I want to ask him about a friend of mine by the name of Danny Miller."

That caused the old man's bushy eyebrows to scrunch together and his lips to curl into a scowl. It was just the sort of reaction that most people got when they thought back to dealing with Danny.

"Wait out back," the old man said. "I'll tell Ernesto you're here."

"All right. Then—"

Before Clint could finish what he was saying, the door was slammed in his face. If he'd taken half a step more, he might have had a part of him wedged in the door and lost forever, since the old man had put a bit of muscle into closing it.

When he turned around, Clint saw Lyssa doing a bad job of keeping herself from laughing at him. He held up a finger, warning her to keep right on trying to suppress her amusement. Lyssa bit on her lower lip and followed Clint as he walked around the building.

In a strange way, the backside of the building was much more appealing than the front. It could have been that the porch was wide open and looked out onto a beautiful stretch of sandy hills. It could also have been that the rear portion of the building had been built from wood that hadn't been through a fire.

"How long should we wait here?" Lyssa asked.

"Shouldn't be long."

Wrapping her arms around herself, she said, "I don't like it here, Clint. These men are looking at me like they've never seen a woman before."

"You wanted to come along on this trip," he reminded her. "If you'd rather have me take you home, I'll be more than happy to."

Lyssa squared her shoulders and fixed Clint with a determined stare. Suddenly, that stare took on a whole new meaning as her eyes went wide and her mouth opened in surprise.

Clint had about half a second to react. He couldn't see what had caused the sudden change in Lyssa's face, but he sure as hell knew it wasn't him. Since she was gaping at something over his left shoulder, he turned in that direction.

With his fist clenched into a tight ball, Clint twisted at the hip and strained his neck to get a look at what was coming his way. The impact of boots against the boards under his feet told him that someone was coming up behind him real quickly. When he got a look at the face that was intent on ambushing him, Clint unleashed the punch he'd been holding back until the very last minute.

Clint's arm snapped forward like a coiled spring, sending his fist around in a tight arc. It sailed right past his face and into the face of the man who was rushing up behind him. The impact made a loud crunch and sent a good amount of pain through both men.

The punch caught the other man in the side of his face, sending him into an awkward sidestep. Since his knuckles mashed against cheekbone, Clint felt as if he'd tried to punch a jagged piece of timber. It wasn't poetry in motion, but it bought enough time for Clint to turn around and face his would-be attacker.

"Who the hell are y—" was all Clint got out before the other man gritted his teeth and came rushing at him again.

The man was shorter than Clint by at least a few inches. It was difficult to say for certain because he was now hunkering down and charging with both arms outstretched. One side of his narrow face was already swelling up from the punch, giving his dark skin a slightly rosier hue.

Clint knew it was too late to avoid what was coming, but he was able to lift both arms over his head to keep them from getting trapped in the other man's grasp. The guy's shoulder impacted dead center in Clint's torso, driving him back a few steps while forcing most of the wind from his lungs.

Before Clint's back hit the nearest wall, a series of quick jabs were rattling against his ribs. They weren't enough to break a bone with just one shot, but they were already combining into a painful mix.

Clenching his fists once more, Clint drove his left elbow straight down into the other man's back. The right elbow dropped a second later, landing squarely between the man's shoulder blades. Although the barrage of punches to his ribs wasn't stopping, Clint could feel it easing up a bit. He took advantage of that by lifting his right leg straight up until he felt his knee pound into the attacker's chest.

The punches to Clint's ribs stopped. In their place, he could hear the other man pulling in a strained, wheezing breath. Clint put his hands on the man's shoulders and pushed him back. It allowed both of them to take a moment to catch their breath.

Now that he wasn't under direct attack, Clint was able to feel the result of all the punches he'd absorbed. Every breath sent sharp pains through his sides, which didn't get much better when he hacked the air out again.

"What the . . . hell is . . . th :?" Clint asked between gasps.

The dark-skinned man looked up at Clint. His features appeared to be Mexican, but with a more angular look. His hair was dark as a horse's mane and seemed to be just as coarse. "Tell Farnsworth to go to the devil!" he spat. "He won't get no more from me."

Now that he'd had a chance to take a breath, Clint straightened up and took a look around. There were some others looking on, but none of them seemed too eager to jump into the fray. "I don't work for Farnsworth."

"No?"

"No. I'm looking for Ernesto."

The other man's breath paused for a moment, only to be let out in a hacking laugh. "Well then, you found him."

FOURTEEN

Most of Clint's muscles were still tensed to continue the fight. Fortunately, his reflexes were good enough to keep those muscles in check.

"Ernesto?" Clint asked, just to make sure that he'd heard the other man correctly. "You're Ernesto?"

The Mexican appeared to be in the same state of readiness as Clint. His fists were still balled and his eyes watched every one of Clint's moves. "*Sí*. I'm Ernesto."

Clint decided to make the next move. Allowing himself to relax was the hard part. Once that was done, approaching Ernesto wasn't all that bad. When he extended his hand, however, he was still getting ready to take a punch to the jaw.

"I'm Clint Adams."

After a few wary moments, Ernesto followed suit and shook Clint's hand. "You already know my name, señor."

"Yeah, but I'm not too sure on why you jumped me."

Ernesto shrugged and said, "I see the gun you're wearing and maybe jump to conclusions. Lately, strangers with guns haven't meant good things for Ernesto."

"I know how that feels."

"And who is this?" Ernesto asked, glancing over to Lyssa.

Before Clint could make any introductions, Lyssa stepped forward and offered her hand. "My name's Lyssa Olam. I'm a reporter for the *Jenegal Gazette*."

By the look in his eye, the words that came out of her mouth weren't even half as interesting as the mouth itself. Like most of the others in the small town, Ernesto watched her like a coyote waiting for the right moment to pounce.

If Lyssa noticed this, she gave no sign. Instead, she shook his hand and kept right on talking.

"We're here to see what you know about a man named Danny Miller," she said. "I've heard that you're the man to talk to regarding that one. I'd really appreciate hearing about whatever you can tell me about him."

As Lyssa spoke, her voice became sweet as honey and even a little bit flirtatious. It seemed that she not only knew what was going through Ernesto's mind, but was using it to her advantage like a seasoned professional.

As much as Ernesto wanted to keep looking at her, the Mexican snapped himself out of his stupor once he heard Danny's name. Suddenly, he looked around at all the faces staring at the three of them from the surrounding area.

"I got nothing to say about that," Ernesto grunted. Keeping his eyes fixed on Clint, he motioned with his head toward the open door nearby. "I don't know any Danny Miller. I keep to my business and that's all." Once again, he motioned toward the door. *"Buenos tardes."*

With that, Ernesto pushed past Clint and Lyssa so he could walk through the door that he'd been eyeing moments ago. He slammed it behind him with such force that the door rattled on its hinges before swinging lazily back and forth.

"I guess this is a dead end," Clint said. He could tell that Lyssa was going to protest, but took her hand and pulled her along before she could say a word.

Even without taking a good look around, Clint could tell the onlookers were finding other things to do. It was similar to the feeling a man got when a storm passed overhead. The clouds may still have been there, but the immediate danger had passed.

Clint pushed open the door and stepped inside with Lyssa right behind him. The room was awash with shadows that were sliced up by the sunlight that cut through the walls. Dust swirled in the air, growing thicker with every one of Clint's steps.

At the back of the room, Ernesto was lowering himself down onto a tall stool. Clint could tell by the way the Mexican was positioned and how he was sitting that Ernesto was ready to draw his gun at any time. That suited Clint just fine.

"Did anyone see you come in here?" Ernesto asked.

Clint nodded and said, "Probably."

After a moment, Ernesto waved an impatient hand toward the door that they'd all just used. "Eh, forget them. I'm tired of watching every last set of eyes in this place."

"So, I take it there's no love lost between you and this Farnsworth person?"

Hearing that name was enough to make the hackles stand up on the back of Ernesto's neck. "You could say that. If I made a mistake about you, I am sorry. If I didn't, you made a big mistake coming in here."

Clint made himself comfortable on one of the other stools in the room. Holding his hands out, he said, "I don't even know who Farnsworth is. Like I said, we're looking for Danny Miller. Have you ever met him?"

"Sí. Pale gringo with a lot of guns. I've seen him."

"How long ago?"

"About a month. Maybe less. I took him to meet a ship that was headed south."

"What ship?" Clint asked, feeling like a miner who'd just spotted a glint of gold after chipping through layers of stubborn, worthless rock.

"It was called *The White Crow* and it was docked right at the coast straight west from here."

"Is it a dangerous ride?"

Ernesto cocked his head as a sly grin crept onto his face. "You're thinking your friend with the guns wouldn't have needed Ernesto just to meet a boat, eh?"

Clint nodded. "Something like that."

"It's only a dangerous ride if you take the wrong path. Plenty of banditos out there. Even a few who would kill you just for the sport. But your friend, he was interested in some of those, as well."

"That sounds like Danny."

Tired of waiting for the conversation to swing in the right direction, Lyssa spoke up. "Can you take us to where you took Danny?"

Ernesto looked over at her with renewed interest. After a few moments of drinking in the sight of her, he nodded. "I can take you. I'll even charge you a smaller fee. That is, if señorita will give a little something to me."

"We'll pay the same fee," Lyssa said. "Even a little more, since there's two of us. Right, Clint?"

"Are you always so quick to hand out other people's money?" Clint asked.

Lyssa threw a mortified look at Clint, which didn't fade much even after he'd started laughing.

"We'll pay the fee, Ernesto," Clint said. "Plus a bit more if the conversation takes an interesting turn during the ride."

Ernesto's nod was subtle and very grateful. Although he tried to look at ease, every moment he sat in that room with Clint and Lyssa was wearing away on him. When he got up, he looked as though he might draw his gun right then and there.

"Take your conversation and shove it up your ass, gringo," Ernesto said loudly. "That's what you get for my fee. And if you don't pay, Ernesto will kill you both."

When he was within arm's reach of Clint, Ernesto leaned down and whispered, "Start riding west and I'll catch up to you in about ten miles."

Clint nodded.

"Oh, and one more thing," Ernesto added with a smirk. "Try to look scared on your way out."

FIFTEEN

Ten miles outside of town, Clint and Lyssa were waiting in a clearing just off the trail. The clearing was big enough for the horses to stand comfortably, but was small enough to go unnoticed by anyone not looking for it as they rode by. Of course, not too many people were looking for them as they rode by.

In fact, nobody rode by until Ernesto came along.

The Mexican was moving at an even pace, studying every inch of terrain as he went. It was plain to see that he knew the area like the back of his hand, since he looked for Clint and Lyssa in a few places that Clint hadn't even seen when he'd come along that same path. In no time at all, Ernesto spotted the other two and rode for them.

"Sorry if I was rude, my friends," Ernesto said. "But Perro Poco isn't a very friendly town."

Lyssa smiled and rode out first to meet him. "It's all right. Anyplace named after a puppy can't be that bad."

The lecherous smile came onto Ernesto's face almost instantly. "Puppy? You think the town was named after a puppy?" Looking over to Clint, he got a roll of the eyes in response. "It's named after a dish served to the mayor just before he was chased out of the country. He asked if it was a little beef tossed into his stew and he found out it was a little dog. A little bit of his own dog, is more like it."

Ernesto broke into a laugh that sounded as if it were shredding the back of his throat.

Lyssa's smile had become nothing but a pale reflection on her face.

"Let's get going," Clint said. "I don't think Danny's got enough time for us to be joking around like this."

"Oh, your friend may have all the time in the world, señor."

"What's that supposed to mean?"

"He was going after Farnsworth," Ernesto replied matter-of-factly. "That means he's probably already dead or locked up somewhere that even the Good Lord might forget about him." Shrugging, he added, "The jungles down there are even less friendly than Perro Poco."

The look on Clint's face was easy enough to interpret. He wanted to get moving and wasn't in the mood for any more lollygagging.

Picking up on that with no trouble, Ernesto shrugged and snapped his reins. "This is the way we went, señor. Are you interested in the quickest way or the way to check in on some of the bounties your friend was after?"

"Did you take him all the way to that boat?"

"Sí."

"Then that's where I want to go. The quicker the better."

After giving Lyssa one more wink, Ernesto steered his horse back onto the trail and got moving. Clint fell into step beside him and Lyssa hung back just enough to keep their guide where she could see him. It wasn't until a half hour later that any of them felt like talking.

"So, who's this Farnsworth I keep hearing so much about?" Clint asked.

"Ah," Ernesto said, "I suppose this is where that extra fee comes in?"

"Depends on how much you can tell me."

Ernesto started to say something, but stopped himself short. His eyes made a quick glance toward Clint's gun before hopping back up to look at his face. "I think you are the real Clint Adams, no?"

"It's not too healthy for folks to pretend to be me."

"I was thinking the same thing. So, that's why I'll tell you this much for free." Ernesto leaned over in his saddle as if he were about to impart some piece of holy wisdom. "Farnsworth is a dangerous man. You know those banditos that kill for sport? Farnsworth eats them for breakfast. Because of that, Ernesto stays away from him."

After Ernesto had righted himself in his saddle, Clint asked, "Is that all you know about him?"

"It's all I need to know. Men who ask too many questions about Farnsworth wind up like your friend Danny."

"If you know that much about him, then you must know how he got his reputation."

Ernesto looked around as if he thought someone were floating over his shoulder just to listen in on the conversation. All he saw was the trees and hills on either side of the trail. Even so, he still seemed a bit reluctant to talk. "Farnsworth comes here wanting to be a king. He doesn't bother with this country because he knows he can get away with spilling more blood in another.

"He came into Mexico to recruit the men he lost on his way from where he came from."

"And where's that?" Lyssa asked.

Shifting in his saddle, Ernesto leered at her and replied, "England."

"How did Danny get involved with Farnsworth?" Clint asked.

Ernesto took his time turning to face the proper direction once more. "He didn't. At least, not at first. Danny came to Perro Poco asking for a guide into the jungles. After he come back, he start asking about Farnsworth. When nobody have anything to say to him, Danny leaves. He came back later on asking about the quickest way to get into Peru.

"Me and the others in Perro Poco knew he was still after Farnsworth. We were all glad to know that the Englishman had gone into that same place. Danny made a big stink in town, saying he would start bringing in wanted men if he didn't get someone to take him to Peru. I offered to take him as far as I could just to save his life."

By this time, Lyssa had worked her way up to ride next to Clint. That also put her on an even line with Ernesto. "You saved his life?" she asked.

"*Sí*, señorita. There are lots of wanted men in Perro Poco."

"And Danny was willing to pay your fee," Clint pointed out.

"*Sí*," Ernesto said. "He was. So I take him to the boat, take his money and hope that's the last I hear about him or Farnsworth. I figure that if your friend wants to get himself killed, that's his business. I just hoped that he didn't tell Farnsworth that we knew about him in Perro Poco."

"Which is why you came out swinging when we came along," Clint said, more as an explanation for Lyssa.

Now, Ernesto turned to look at Clint with an apologetic shrug. "Right," he said. "That's why I come out swinging. So, is that an interesting conversation?"

"It'll do," Clint replied with a nod. He then started to dig in his pocket for some money. What he heard next was almost enough of a surprise to knock him off of Eclipse's back.

"Keep the money, señor. I want to come with you, instead."

SIXTEEN

Before Clint could say anything to that, Lyssa practically lunged across him.

"You want to do *what*?" she asked. To Clint, she said, "We don't need anyone else coming along for this. There's plenty of guides to hire once we get there."

"But none of them know the jungles like me, señorita. There are jungles in Mexico, but not like the ones you'll see when that boat pulls up and drops you into Peru. I was raised in jungles like those. Ernesto knows where to step and where not to step. Without knowing that, you will be dead in two days."

"We don't need a guide," Lyssa said to Ernesto. "You took enough of our money. You've been a great help. I'm sure Clint doesn't want anyone tagging along with us."

Clint pulled back on his reins and brought Eclipse to a stop. On either side of him, Lyssa and Ernesto had to stop and then back up a few steps to get back to where he was waiting.

"Before you two start going on much longer about what I should say," Clint snarled, "how about if I actually get to say something, first?"

Ernesto and Lyssa looked at Clint as if he'd just rapped

them both on their noses. Then, they eased back into their saddles.

"Good." Looking first to Ernesto, Clint said, "You coming with us farther than the dock was never part of the deal."

"I know, but you will need a guide when you get to where you're going."

"Then why didn't you mention anything about that in the first place?"

"Because I needed to be sure I could trust you."

Clint's eyes narrowed and he studied the other man carefully. "What makes you think you can trust us now?"

Ernesto didn't flinch under Clint's glare. In fact, he gave a little of it right back to him. "I don't. What I do know is that you're not working for Farnsworth."

"Yeah? How's that?"

"Because anyone on his payroll would have killed me by now for what I said."

Although he wasn't convinced 100 percent, Clint didn't think the other man was outright lying to him. "And if Farnsworth is as bad as you say he is, why would you want to come with us? Sounds to me like you're pretty safe right where you are."

"Safe is one thing, señor. Rich is another." Leaning forward in his saddle, Ernesto said, "I know about the gold."

By saying that, Clint knew that the other man had just proven himself a bit more. If Clint was in league with anyone after that money who wasn't trustworthy, he would have killed Ernesto then and there. Plenty of men had been killed to keep a halfway valuable claim under a greedy miner's hat. Gold country was filled with more corpses than nuggets for that very reason.

Ernesto's hand had once again drifted to the gun at his side. When he saw Clint nod, he moved his hand away from his gun. Apparently, he'd liked what he'd seen, too.

"Danny told you about the treasure?" Lyssa asked as though she could scarcely believe it.

"He did, señorita. But I don't think he meant to. I overheard him talking to a man he met at the dock."

"Overheard," Clint asked, "or eavesdropped?"

Ernesto merely shrugged at the accusation. "Does it matter? What matters is what I heard."

"Which was what?" When he saw that the answer wasn't forthcoming, Clint put more of an edge in his voice. "Come on, Ernesto. I don't have the time to keep playing word games with you. Either tell me or don't. Stop wasting my time."

"The man your friend talked to was the last man who talked to him," Ernesto said. "At least, he was the last one that I ever saw."

"And what did he say?"

Ernesto looked back and forth between Clint and Lyssa, who were both leaning forward, eagerly awaiting a response. Letting out a breath, Ernesto said, "He said that Farnsworth was already sitting on a pile of gold."

"Aw, hell." Clint grunted. "That means Danny is probably dead already."

"Maybe not, señor. I don't think your friend was surprised to hear about this. He said that he would come back with Farnsworth in one hand and that gold in the other. He said he had a plan. And if he already went down there carrying all those guns, I'll bet there's still plenty of smoke in the air for us to follow right back to your friend."

"And to the gold," Lyssa pointed out in an accusing tone of voice.

"Sure," Ernesto said unapologetically. "They shouldn't be too far from each other."

"That was a while ago," Clint said by way of thinking out loud.

"Some gringo comes down to pick a fight with a man like Farnsworth over a pile of gold," Ernesto said. "That is a story that will be told by the locals down there for years to come."

Lyssa's excitement was growing by the second. That much could be seen in the way she practically stood up in her stirrups with every other breath. "It's a story everyone across the country will want to read!"

But no matter how excited the other two became, Clint was still wearing the same thoughtful expression that had been on his face the entire time. Lyssa looked over to him as if she couldn't believe what she was seeing.

"You can't sit there and tell me you don't want to see this through," she said breathlessly.

"I want to see it through," he said. "I just don't want to be the one to tell Danny's wife and three little girls that he went and got himself killed chasing after some fairy tale."

SEVENTEEN

They rode straight to the coast and straight through the night. Ernesto was in the lead the entire time, leading Clint and Lyssa onto paths that neither of them would have even known existed unless they'd been shown them firsthand. Even then, there were a few turns where it seemed as if Ernesto was veering off for no reason.

Following their guide, Clint and Lyssa somehow found themselves on a sorry excuse for a trail that shaved a few hours off their travel time. It didn't take long before even Lyssa was putting her faith in the Mexican. Clint, on the other hand, made sure to keep both of them where he could see them.

It wasn't until they caught the scent of salt in the air that they gave their horses a rest and allowed them to walk rather than run. After cresting the next rise, all three of them had their breath taken away by the sight of the ocean spread out in front of them like a giant, swaying blanket of blue.

The docks were in sight. They weren't much more than a few sticks that managed to float on top of the giant, undulating mass that was the Pacific Ocean. Clint and Lyssa

had to take a moment to adjust themselves to the sudden
appearance of so much water.

Ernesto had yet to look over his shoulder before select-
ing his path and riding toward the dock.

"Does Danny Miller really have a wife and three girls?"
Lyssa asked.

Clint nodded. "His wife's name is Sabrina. The girls are
Grace, Sydney and Peyton. Cutest little faces you'd ever
want to see."

She smiled at him. Actually, she smiled more at the
smirk that had come onto Clint's face when he mentioned
those little girls. "I didn't know about Miller's family."

The smile on Clint's face faded a bit when he looked
over at her. "Did you ever really check into it? Seemed to
me like you or any of those other reporters could only see
the guns he wore or the fights Danny got himself into."

"I guess that's true. How do you know so much?"

"Because I know Danny Miller and I bothered to take a
moment to see what kind of man he is. I don't exactly want
to put my life on the line for some stack of gold that's probably just the figment of some drunk's imagination. But
everyone leaves someone behind, Lyssa. Even bounty
hunters. Just because they're left behind doesn't mean
those little girls need to grow up without their father."

Clint watched Lyssa from the corner of his eye. Although it hadn't been his intention, he wondered if what
he'd said would have any impact on the reporter.

She was looking at him for a few quiet moments and
then shifted her eyes to the ocean. After letting out a
breath, Lyssa faced Clint once more and said, "I'll be sure
to include some family history in my story. You can tell me
all about it once we get on that ship. I'll race you!"

With that, Lyssa snapped her reins and went charging
off to catch up with Ernesto.

Clint had to shake his head at how single-minded some

people could be. Of course, much of what he knew on that matter came from personal experience, so he couldn't exactly cast too many aspersions.

All that mattered in the end was that the right thing got done. Different folks would have their different reasons for walking their path, but so long as the path was a good one the rest usually had a tendency to work itself out.

He hadn't been lying about Danny's family. Clint had only met them once, but had heard about them every single time he and Danny had crossed paths. Whatever else he might be, Danny Miller was true to his family. No man was a good enough liar to cover up the spark that came into Danny's eyes whenever he'd talked about that wife and those kids.

Until now, Clint had been thinking of that family when he'd kept their existence to himself. Danny had always done the same, knowing full well that the men a bounty hunter crossed would like nothing more than to know a weak spot on their enemy.

A pretty little family waiting for Danny's return was a major weak spot in the eyes of killers and vengeful thieves. Since it was too late to change Danny's way of life, the most Clint could hope for was to give the fellow a second chance.

Every man deserved that much.

Besides, it had been a long while since Clint had last been on the ocean.

EIGHTEEN

The docks that Ernesto had brought them to were much more impressive when viewed from afar. Up close, they appeared to be no more than a rickety boardwalk supported by moldy posts stretching out onto the water.

There was one boat tethered to the dock with its sails currently tied down in dirty bundles around the masts. A few men walked here and there, on and off the boat. As far as Clint could tell, they were carrying crates and various dry goods from the ship's hold to be loaded onto a pair of wagons that had made it dockside moments before Clint arrived.

Lyssa and Ernesto were already off their horses and walking down the dock when Clint climbed down from Eclipse and tied the Darley Arabian next to the rest of the horses. The moment Clint's boots touched the ground, the hard ride from Perro Poco made itself known in his legs, all the way up through his shoulders. He was still working out the kinks when he caught up to Lyssa.

"Where's Ernesto going?" Clint asked as he watched their guide walk all the way to the end of the docks so he could wave his arms at some of the passing sailors.

"He went to try and find the captain," Lyssa replied.

"I've had enough of being gawked at by lonely men, so I let him go right ahead."

"You've had enough? And here I thought you were going to try and get us a better rate for passage the way only you could."

Lyssa's arm swept out and caught Clint on the shoulder. The look on her face told him that she was more than willing to follow that smack up with another. "Keep it up and even you won't get to get the things that only I can deliver."

Clint smirked and rubbed his shoulder. "Fair enough, but I'd still like to get in on whatever is being said over there."

Lyssa snapped her head around to look at what Ernesto was doing. Sure enough, the dark-skinned man had found a sailor who wasn't too busy unloading the ship to talk to him. At the moment, both men were engaged in a conversation that involved plenty of hand motions and waving back and forth toward Clint and Lyssa.

"Stay here," Clint said.

Before Lyssa could reply, Clint was already walking down the dock. He could still see her as he made his way, but getting closer to the boat made it seem as if he was already a mile away from her. Part of that could have been due to the way the ground suddenly gave way to water and floating boards under his feet. Another part could have been the static in the air, which came from the constant flow of motion on and off the boat.

The boat itself wasn't too impressive. It bobbed on the water like a cork, but groaned like an old woman complaining under her breath at having to climb a flight of stairs. A set of planks lashed together with ropes was spanning the gap between the boat and the dock. Although those planks were creaking louder than the rest, the bulky sailors carried their loads over them as if the planks were made of stone.

As Clint approached the two conversing men, he saw

the sailor's eyes lock onto him suspiciously. Ernesto looked over his shoulder, saw Clint approaching and then threw himself back into his negotiations.

"It's got to be all three of us," Ernesto said. "That's the deal."

"We don't have that kind of room," the sailor replied, still watching Clint like a hawk. "Not unless you want to wait for *White* to come back."

"We can't wait. That's what I'm trying to tell you."

"Is there a problem?" Clint asked before Ernesto could throw himself into a full tirade.

The sailor was big man who was built like several slabs of beef lashed together in a fashion similar to the planks leading off the dock. His black hair hung in awkwardly cut clumps, framing a wide face, which was currently twisted into an aggravated grimace.

Dressed in dark clothes that were every bit as weathered as the boat behind him, he looked like a cross between a tired cowboy and a pirate. The sailor regarded Clint with weary apprehension. Although there wasn't any threat in his dark eyes just yet, that could obviously change in a heartbeat. "Who the hell are you?"

"I'm with Ernesto here. The name's Clint."

"You fellas some kind of wanted men?" the sailor asked.

"Not hardly. We just need to get down to Peru."

"Tumbes," Ernesto corrected. He looked over to Clint and nodded. "We need to get to Tumbes."

Hearing that, the sailor's eyes narrowed and he looked over both Clint and Ernesto with renewed intensity. Those eyes stopped on Ernesto and stayed there as he said, "I've seen you before."

"*Sí, sí*. I've been through here many times."

"And you were with another armed man back then. Armed to the teeth. Said he was a hunter."

"*Sí, sí*."

"What about this one here?" the sailor asked, nodding toward Clint. "You saying he's a hunter, too?" When Ernesto didn't shoot back an immediate response, the sailor disregarded him altogether. Turning his sharp gaze to Clint, he said, "You look like a wanted man to me. Normally I don't have much objection to taking passengers, no matter who they are, but that's changed lately."

"I'm not a wanted man," Clint said. "I just need to get where I'm going as quickly as I can."

"We're not taking any passengers," the sailor growled. "Not you three, anyway."

Clint could feel the anger working its way up from the bottom of his stomach into the back of his throat. Rather than spit that anger out to its source, he nodded and took a few breaths to calm himself. "Where's the captain of this boat?"

"I'm the captain of both the boats that dock here, *White* and *Gray*. John Layfield. You want to book passage, you either go through me or hike down the coast yourselves."

Clint looked at the side of the boat, where faded letters painted onto the side marked it as *The Gray Crow*. According to Ernesto, Danny Miller had taken *The White Crow* into Peru.

Behind Captain Layfield, the other sailors chuckled and wandered up closer to the dock. Some of them were cracking their knuckles while others were reaching for various weapons. Every one of them looked ready for a fight. All they needed was word from their captain or some other halfway convenient excuse.

NINETEEN

Since the casual approach wasn't working too well, Clint decided to be a little more direct. He stepped up to Captain Layfield until he was almost toe to toe with the man. The other men on the dock had already stopped what they were doing to watch what would happen next.

Staring up into the bigger man's eyes, Clint kept his hand away from his gun. "That other man you were talking about," Clint said evenly, "the one with all the guns. He's the one I'm after."

Captain Layfield nodded while motioning for the rest of his men to keep their distance for the moment. "All right."

"I need to get to him and I can't let any more time pass before I do, so we need to work something out between you and I."

Layfield gnawed on his bottom lip as he thought that over. "Turn over your guns and we can work something out."

"You know I'd be stupid to do that."

As with most negotiations, the first offer was never a serious one and Captain Layfield only nodded as he thought about it some more. "Let the woman bunk down with me and it's a deal."

77

The angry fire in Clint's eyes was all the captain needed to see to know that offer was rejected.

Finally, Layfield let out a sigh and started rubbing his chin. Only now did he truly look over the new arrivals to the dock. "All three of you need to go?"

"Yes, sir."

"And the horses?"

"As many as possible."

"All right, then. All of you can go for a thousand dollars. All three horses, too."

Clint knew a bum steer when he saw one and was impressed that Captain Layfield managed to keep a straight face when he put the offer on the table. Fortunately for Clint, not all of the other sailors nearby were so talented. Some of those men were smirking to themselves, which told Clint that he was definitely about to get hung out to dry.

Suddenly, Clint had to fight back a smirk of his own. "What kind of fees do you pay to dock down in Peru?"

That caught Layfield off his guard. "Fees are included."

"I'll bet they are. And that cargo your men are unloading is all strictly legal, right?"

Captain Layfield's hands had been steady at his sides until now. When he heard Clint's question, he made a subtle move for something tucked under his waistband beneath his shirt. Clint's hand drifted a little closer to his modified Colt, which stopped the captain cold.

"You the law?" Layfield asked.

"Not at all."

"Then you can keep your nose out of what I choose to fill my ship with. In fact, you and your horses can turn around and take your sorry asses away from my dock."

"My guess is that the fees you pay are at least double what they should be."

"Closer to triple."

"And I'd also wager that they're not being charged by anyone with real authority to do so," Clint continued.

The edge quickly vanished from Layfield's expression. Although he didn't say anything, everything else about him told Clint that he was interested in hearing more.

Clint didn't exactly whisper, but he wasn't speaking loudly enough for anyone beyond himself, the captain and Ernesto to overhear what he was saying. "If you just had to pay whatever the real rates are for using the docks or getting supplies or whatever you need, I'll bet you'd clear a hell of a lot more profit in the long run."

Layfield's laugh was more of a grunting snort. "Wouldn't be long at all before I see more profit if that happened."

"And if that were to happen, would it be worth the price for me, my friends and our horses to be taken to . . ."

Although he'd been enthralled with the bargaining process going on in front of him, Ernesto quickly sensed when he was needed to step in. "Tumbes. We need to go to Tumbes."

"Right," Clint said. "Would it be worth passage for all of us to Tumbes and back again?"

"Maybe."

"I bet it would even be worth it if I was bringing back another passenger with me."

"How many more?" Layfield asked.

"Should be just one."

Although he'd been considering what Clint was saying, Captain Layfield gritted his teeth and let out another grunt. "Bullshit. You don't even know what fees I need to pay."

"That's true. But I do know who would benefit the most from bringing those fees up so high that you can't even afford to take care of your boats."

Layfield grinned, knowing well enough that he'd called Clint's bluff and was once again on top of the heap. "Who?"

"Fellow by the name of Farnsworth?"

The smile dropped off of Captain Layfield's mouth in the blink of an eye. "What's that name mean to you?"

"It's the name of a murdering thief who thinks he's royalty in those jungles," Clint said. "And it's also the name of a man who's probably surrounded himself with enough guns that he can charge whatever he wants to hardworking men like yourself who just want to make a living.

"It may be the name of the man supplying you with some of your cargo, but I'll bet you're too smart to think that he's doing anything but stealing from you, just as he's stealing from everyone else he meets."

Layfield nodded just enough for it to be seen. "What's any of that got to do with our business?"

"I'm going down to Peru to have a word with Mister Farnsworth. While I'm there, I can take care of those fees as well as tie up some other matters that can do nothing but make things easier for you. Take us down there and back and you'll benefit immediately."

"How do I know you can do any of that?"

"Send some of your men along with us when we get there. I'll need a guide who knows where Farnsworth operates anyhow. If I stray, your men can set me right. If I can't deliver, they can drag me back to answer to you personally."

Clint relaxed his posture a bit and dropped his voice to a more conversational tone. "Look, I'm not stupid enough to lie to you now just so I can sail on a boat with you and your crew and stab you in the back once I get to a jungle that would swallow me whole in a matter of minutes. We can help each other here. We can stay in a hold or whatever space you've got. Honestly, unless you plan on running with the ship packed all the way to the top with cargo headed for Peru, you've got nothing to lose."

Captain Layfield took another look at Clint, Ernesto and Lyssa. This time, however, he seemed to be sizing them up the way a cattle baron sized up a group of steers. His eyes wound up back on Clint and stayed there. "You know I'll kill you if you even think about putting one over on me?"

Clint nodded.

"And I'll take that pretty thing over there and keep her until her face ain't so pretty no more," Layfield added.

"That won't be necessary," Clint said.

After another few moments, Layfield nodded. "All right, then. We're pulling out in the morning. You want to come along, you'll help us with the loading and unloading. I intend on getting something out of this one way or another."

"You heard the man," Clint said to Ernesto. "Let's get to work."

TWENTY

The village wasn't alone in its stretch of jungle, but it might as well have been, for all the contact it had with its neighbors. Although the closest settlement was only a few miles away, those miles in between them were filled with enough vegetation to make every step a chore in itself.

Trees stood so close together that they formed a living wall that surrounded the village on all sides. It was the duties of the younger children and older villagers to keep the jungle at bay. It was the men's duty to travel into the wilds on a daily basis and it was no strange occurrence for some of those men to disappear into the jungle forever.

As of the last year or two, disappearances like that were becoming more and more frequent. While men had fallen victim to hungry animals or poisons dripping from countless flowers, the majority of local casualties were being taken by predators of a two-legged variety.

In fact, a pack of those very predators was chopping its way into the village at this very moment.

The hacking sounds of blades through branches mixed into the rest of the noises of the jungle until the very last minute. Once the villagers picked up on that sound, they could already see the trees shaking and spitting out the men dressed in filthy uniforms of thick brown cotton.

As soon as the first man stepped out of the trees, he hefted the machete he'd been using onto his shoulder. His other hand pulled the gun from its holster, which hung at his side. He spotted the closest villager and flashed a gap-toothed smile.

"Tell your chief Mister Farnsworth is here," the man with the machete said in a thick accent that sounded like twanging strings.

On either side of the first man, others dressed in similar colors stepped out from the trees. There were nine in all and the last few to arrive flanked a slender, older man who strode with his head held high. Already, the jungle was closing up to cover their entrance.

That part of the village was a section with only a few huts that kept their backs to the jungle. In this area, there were only a small child and an elderly woman sitting on a rickety stoop, weaving narrow leaves into the shapes of baskets.

The child looked over to the old woman with wide, frightened eyes.

"Go on," the woman said in the dialect of her village. "Do what the man says."

The man standing in the center of the uniformed gunmen watched the child scamper off with an approving nod. Graham Farnsworth was like an old photograph. He was gray around the edges and black at his core. Cold eyes took in the world around him without blinking. A hooked nose came down like a beak in the middle of his face and tufts of white hair stuck out like bristles from beneath the hat perched atop his head.

"That child obeys very nicely." Looking around at the backside of the village, Farnsworth didn't even try to hide the contemptuous sneer on his face. "Too bad the rest of you lot aren't so easily trained."

The old woman barely even acknowledged the group that had stepped out from the jungle. Although there were paths established leading into the foliage, such unannounced entrances didn't seem to be much of a surprise to her.

Within seconds, the child returned. Her hand was wrapped around that of a large man dressed in brown pants and a brightly colored poncho. He rushed forward and immediately scooped the child to one side the moment he spotted Farnsworth and his men.

"We're here for the taxes," the uniformed man with the machete announced.

After pulling in a breath to steady himself, the man in the poncho stepped forward with his arms outstretched. "Señor Farnsworth, my people are poor. We barely have the means to stay alive. We cannot pay your taxes."

"Am I not generous in allowing you to trade with other villages?" Farnsworth asked. "Do I not grant you safe passage through a jungle which I, personally, cleared of bandits?"

It was common knowledge that those bandits were mostly now in Farnsworth's employ. As that went through his mind, the man in the poncho found himself glancing over to the thug carrying the machete.

That thug responded with a cruel snarl.

"Y . . . yes," the man in the poncho said.

"Then what is the excuse for you not being able to pay your taxes?" Farnsworth asked. "If you can make a living, trade freely and go where you please, then you must be making enough money to sustain yourselves. This child here looks healthy enough to me."

As if reading the Englishman's thoughts, the man with the machete lunged forward to grab hold of the child by her neck. When the man in the poncho started to react, he was instantly stopped by two more of Farnsworth's group.

"My constables are fair men," Farnsworth said. "But they are not going to do your work for you. They need to eat just as you do and without taxes, they are forced to suffer." Farnsworth looked down at the child as if he were forcing himself to look a pig in the eyes. "It's best for you to see how the world works for yourself. That way, perhaps you can avoid making these same mistakes."

"Señor Farnsworth, please. I just need a little more—"

"You've had plenty of time to collect the money, Topac," Farnsworth interrupted. "Since you don't have it now, I must assume that you never meant to pay me."

"That's not true! What you ask is too much! Just a little more time! That's all we need."

"What you need is to learn a lesson." Farnsworth knelt down so he was on the little girl's level. "Nothing is free in this world. Whatever you want, you need to pay the price." He stood up, clasped his hands behind his back and said, "My constables will now collect what you owe however they see fit. Next time taxes are due and you don't feel like paying, you and these people had better start looking for a cave to live in."

Before Topac could say another word, Farnsworth snapped his fingers loudly. The men around him surged into the village like a plague of locusts. Doors were kicked in, possessions were looted and screams filled the air all the way into the night.

TWENTY-ONE

After a hard day's work carrying crates and sacks of dry goods from one spot to another, Clint and Ernesto didn't much care where they slept. They rented a squalid little closet that was called a room and that was good enough for them. As long as it had enough space for them to lie down and stretch out their legs, they could have slept in a water trough.

As for Lyssa, she was supposed to have spent the day cleaning the deck of *The Gray Crow* and getting food supplies squared away for the voyage south. In fact, she'd spent just enough time doing that work to convince Captain Layfield that she was holding up her end of the bargain. The rest of her time was spent exploring the ship from stem to stern.

When morning came, Clint and Ernesto were shaken awake. Clint opened his eyes to find Lyssa looking down at him as anxiously as a kid on Christmas morning. She was pulling on her clothes, which made Clint realize just how tired he'd been, since he didn't recall sharing a bed with her.

He and Ernesto looked around at the room as if it were the first time they'd seen it. Neither of them bothered getting acquainted with their surroundings since they were just about to leave them behind.

After stuffing some cold oatmeal down their throats, the three of them followed Captain Layfield's lead and finished loading *The Gray Crow*. Along with their three horses, they brought on a few goats, some cows and even a few crates of chickens. After that, *The Gray Crow* was casting off and leaving the coast behind.

Amazingly enough, Clint got his first real chance to relax once the boat was surrounded by ocean on all sides and the wind had filled her sails. One of the crew nodded toward a pair of rooms that would be theirs for the length of the trip. They were a little smaller than the one they'd rented on land, but at least there were two of them.

Clint took a second and a half to walk around the room and sat down on the edge of a bunk that was hinged onto the wall. "This isn't too bad," he said. "Ernesto even gets his own room."

"I am the lady here," Lyssa pointed out as she leaned against the wall with her arms folded. "Don't you think I should get my own room?"

Smirking, Clint shrugged and said, "Whatever you like. Considering how many men were undressing you with their eyes, I think it's real brave of you to want to sleep in a room alone."

The scowl on Lyssa's face meant that she was all too aware of the looks she'd been getting from Layfield and his crew. To say they'd just been undressing her in those stares was being awfully generous.

Rather than mention that, however, Lyssa gave Clint a shrug in return. "I guess this gives us a chance to put our heads together without being spied on. Besides," she added while looking around at the moldy walls and the footstool roped into one corner, "this is actually better than I was expecting."

"Me, too. I thought we'd be tossed into the hold with the animals. I guess Captain Layfield has some faith in me, after all."

"And that brings me to something that's been bothering me all day. Just how on earth did you know all those things you were saying to the captain?"

"You mean about Farnsworth?"

She nodded, fixing on Clint with an intrigued spark in her eyes. "About Farnsworth, the fees he was charging, the cargo being hauled, all of that. How did you know just what to say to get us on this boat without paying a cent?"

Rubbing his aching shoulders, Clint said, "You may not have paid anything, but Ernesto and I might have something to say about that."

"Well, you know what I mean."

After letting her stew for a few more seconds, Clint finally gave her what she was after. "First of all, Captain Layfield obviously isn't from around here. He's a Texas boy if I ever saw one. And for him to come all this way to set up his docks when plenty more money could be made up the coast of California, he can't be hauling strictly legal cargo."

"I'm impressed," Lyssa said.

"Now, as the fine, upstanding journalist you are, you should know that I've had plenty of dealings with men like Farnsworth."

Deciding to ignore the sarcastic tone in Clint's voice, Lyssa pointed out, "But you said you've never met him."

"I've heard plenty about him, though. As much as I hate to admit it, sometimes that's enough. At least, it was enough in this case. Obviously, Farnsworth is trying to make some grab for power down in Peru. Whether or not he can do it remains to be seen. But any bully worth his salt will try to muscle into whatever quick and easy ways he can to make some money. Extortion is usually the first step there.

"Cheating shopkeepers out of profits, forcing business-men to pay for protection," Clint said, ticking off each point on his fingers, "and forcing traders to pay for safe passage along their routes. It's all been done plenty of times before and it'll be done plenty more so long as there are men out there willing to push around whoever they can."

"But you mentioned Farnsworth in particular."

Clint held his hand out for a moment before lowering it and lifting both shoulders in a shrug. "I took a guess."

"You guessed?"

"In poker, that's a pretty good strategy."

"And it could have also gotten us killed."

"By Captain Layfield? I don't think so. He's tough, but he's no killer."

"And what if you were wrong?" Lyssa asked.

"Then I would have been forced to pay about triple what these rooms were worth and we'd still be on our way to Peru. The trick with carrying money with you is in making other folks think that you're showing all you've got."

Lyssa thought back to the barkeep Clint had bribed back at the saloon in Perro Poco. Even she'd thought that he'd taken out that wad of bills and just handed them over. The barkeep's eyes had gone wide with greed, proving that he was thinking along those very same lines.

"So you could have afforded to pay for these rooms, outright?" she asked.

Clint nodded. "Sure, but that wouldn't have been any fun. Plus, guessing about what Farnsworth is into is one thing. Knowing that I'm right is another. Captain Layfield told me a hell of a lot."

While she'd gone from looking surprised to shocked to worried, Lyssa was now wearing an expression of genuine admiration. Sidling up closer to Clint, she eased herself onto his lap and wrapped her arms around his neck.

"You'd make one hell of a reporter," she said.

Clint supported her back with one arm and ran his other hand along the side of her leg. Keeping his voice soft and gentle, he said, "Reporters are a cruel, sneaky bunch. I think I'd rather deal with killers and thieves."

Now, Lyssa's eyes widened again and she smacked him on the back of his head. "That is just plain offensive, Clint Adams!"

Clint smirked as his hat was knocked off his head by the playful slap. "It could have been worse. I could have lumped you in with the lawyers."

Shaking her head, Lyssa started working her fingers through Clint's hair. "So, how long before Captain Layfield fetches you to clean out the galley or swab the decks?"

"This is a cargo ship," Clint laughed. "Not Long John Silver's galleon."

"You know what I mean."

"I think Layfield is trying to decide what to make of us. My guess is he truly wants to see if I can deliver on what I promised."

"Good, then maybe we can take some time for ourselves."

TWENTY-TWO

"Did you show them to their cabins?" Layfield asked.

The man who'd entered the room was a burly sailor who stood a few inches shorter than his captain. A scruffy beard covered the bottom portion of his head, which was shaped like a rectangle that had been chipped from a block of wood. He nodded and said, "Them two right across from the brig, just like you told me."

Nodding, Captain Layfield stretched out so his feet reached the stool that was tied to the wall across from him. Like the rest of *The Gray Crow*, the captain's quarters seemed bigger than they actually were. Amenities were kept to a minimum and every inch of space was used wisely.

There were more comforts in that room than anywhere else on board, but that wasn't saying a whole lot. *The Gray Crow* was built to haul cargo of all shapes and sizes. Just under half of that space had been built into crew quarters and a squalid galley, but that still gave the impression that there was more under its decks than what should be possible.

"You sure you don't want us to keep an eye on them?" the sailor asked.

Layfield shook his head. "With the work I put them

through, I'd be surprised if either of them could do much of anything that I need to worry about. Besides, it's too late for them to cause much trouble now."

"What about the woman?"

"If she sticks her head out of there, the men will scare her right back where she belongs."

"And if she still feels like taking a look around?"

"Then she'll regret it."

The threat in Layfield's tone wasn't lost on the sailor. In fact, the sailor put on a wide, expectant grin when he heard those words.

"But I wouldn't get too anxious about her if I were you," the captain warned. "That man I talked to is Clint Adams."

"Huh?"

"He's a gunfighter. I've heard about him plenty and even saw him a few times the last time I was in San Francisco. Hell of a card player, that one. And that iron strapped to his waist ain't just for show."

"You think he can do what he said?" the sailor asked. "About Farnsworth, I mean."

"Normally, I'd say no goddamn way. But seeing as who's making those claims, this might just work out after all."

"The wind's at our backs, but it's still a ways until we get there. What should we do about them passengers until then?"

Captain Layfield scratched at the stubble on his chin and stared as if he were trying to burn a hole through the wall in front of him. The sounds of the boat creaking and water slapping at its sides were the only ones to drift through the musty air.

Finally, Layfield said, "Give them some time to let their guard down and then bring them up here. If they give you any trouble, take down Adams first and then the others. Since they don't look like the sort to have strong sea legs, you men should be able to get the drop on them."

"Aye, sir."

TWENTY-THREE

The wind was most definitely at their backs. Clint could feel as much by the way the boat would lean forward for a moment as the gusts rushed along the outside of the hull. After that brief moment, everything around him would creak again as *The Gray Crow* was carried through the ocean at a quicker pace.

The rocking of the ship had lessened a bit now that their momentum was carrying them forward. But that didn't mean the ride was perfectly smooth. On the contrary, the room was still creaking from side to side and the walls were still getting buffeted by wind and water alike.

Lyssa was sitting on Clint's lap, her arms and legs wrapped around him. As the boat moved, her body moved along with it to form a rhythm that Clint was quick to catch on to. Ever since the ride from Perro Poco had started, Lyssa had taken to wearing jeans and a plain, plaid shirt. But even those baggy clothes weren't enough to hide the supple body under them.

With her hips shifting to accommodate the boat's tilts and sways, Lyssa rode Clint as if she'd been born and raised upon the sea. Her hands were busy pulling open his shirt and even before she'd gotten it completely off of him, she was starting to work at loosening his belt buckles.

Clint had managed to get adjusted to the ocean's movements as well. He was far from being perfectly balanced upon the rocking bunk, but he managed to stay upright while savoring the way the Pacific grinded Lyssa's little body against him.

He undid the buttons of her blouse and pulled it from her shoulders. The camisole she wore underneath was next to go and soon she was swaying topless on him. Her full, rounded breasts bobbed to the rhythm of the sea. By the time Clint's hands cupped her, Lyssa's nipples were rigid against his palms.

She leaned her head back to savor the feel of his hands upon her, smiling as she allowed herself to sway from side to side. When she opened her eyes again, she looked at him hungrily and placed both palms flat against his chest.

Clint allowed himself to be pushed back onto the bunk. His hands slipped down to her waist where he started tugging Lyssa's jeans down over her hips. After a little bit of squirming, they were both naked and lying on the bunk.

Lyssa remained on top of him. Her bare skin was warm against Clint's body as she pressed herself down on top of him. Grabbing hold of the top edge of the bunk, she closed her eyes and wriggled against him in all the right spots.

For a little while, Clint lay back and enjoyed the way the entire room rocked back and forth around them. His hands wandered over Lyssa's body, coming to a rest upon her plump backside. He didn't feel like relaxing for too long, however. Judging by the way Lyssa was moving, she'd lost some of her patience as well.

Lyssa reacted to Clint's touch by positioning herself on top of him. More specifically, she opened her legs a bit more so she could fit Clint's rigid penis into the wet slit between them.

She shifted and teased the tip of his cock with the wet

lips of her pussy. In no time at all, Clint's hands tightened around her backside so he could pull her closer while also lifting his hips up off the bunk.

His erection slid easily inside of her, fitting perfectly within her warm, damp embrace. Lyssa let out a sigh that was as much relieved as it was satiated. Clint kept his hands on her buttocks, guiding her hips as he pumped in and out of her.

Soon, Lyssa pushed herself up so she was sitting upright and looking down at him. She traced a curving line over his chest while slowly grinding her hips in tight circles.

Clint drank in the sight of her trim body on top of him. Lyssa's breasts swayed with the rhythm of the sea, capped by the little pink nipples, which were now harder than ever. After lifting herself up a bit onto her knees, Lyssa got a whole new rhythm underway.

Moving her hands down Clint's chest, she didn't stop until they were almost together at a spot just above his abdomen. Lyssa then leaned forward and locked her eyes onto Clint while squeezing her breasts together in a way that made his eyes grow wide.

"Are you still trying to butter me up for that interview?" Clint asked.

She smiled and started rocking back and forth on his rigid penis. "Now how could you think such a thing?"

"Because I don't know if I could refuse right about now."

Before she could start asking him questions, Clint reached up and pulled Lyssa down close enough for him to kiss her on the lips. He shifted so that they were both lying on their sides upon the bunk. Lyssa's back was against the wall and Clint had a firm grasp on her with both arms.

As he kissed her passionately, Clint thrust between her legs. He moved in and out of her even quicker once she draped one leg over him and pumped her hips right along with him.

Clint's hand moved up and down along Lyssa's back, tracing a line along the curve of her spine all the way down to the plump curve of her buttocks. His other hand moved along her neck, allowing him to massage her there before sliding his fingers through the dark, silky strands of her hair.

If she'd even started to think about Clint's interview, those thoughts were far from Lyssa's mind now. Leaning against the wall, Lyssa arched her back to press herself against him. Their lengthy kiss broke off and she let out a breathy moan as she once again felt every rigid inch slide into her.

The wind gusted on the other side of the wall, making the entire boat groan with the effort of staying together amidst the growing waves. As *The Gray Crow* climbed one such wave, it rocked to one side, taking Clint and Lyssa along for the ride.

When it rocked in the other direction, the boat rolled Clint against Lyssa even harder. His hands took hold of her to shift her body so that she was lying flat upon the bunk. Clint had barely turned to face her before he felt Lyssa's legs wrap around him.

She gazed up at him, watching anxiously as Clint fit himself once again inside of her. A shuddering moan went through her entire body as Clint entered her while also lowering himself down to lie on top of her.

With their bodies pressed so close together, the rocking of the boat had little hold on them. On the contrary, it added to their movements as Clint clutched her tightly and pumped in and out of her with growing intensity.

"Oh god," Lyssa groaned directly into Clint's ear. "Right there. Right in that spot."

She alternated between hanging onto him and grabbing hold of the bunk itself. Both of their bodies were covered in a thin layer of sweat, which had nothing to do with the humidity inside the cabin.

Clint was about to slide off the bunk, but was just able to swing one leg down to the floor and brace himself before doing so. Using that foot for leverage, he began thrusting between Lyssa's thighs even harder. Every time he buried his cock in her, he could feel Lyssa's body tensing and could hear her groaning for more.

Soon, Lyssa was no longer making any noise. Her mouth was open slightly, but no sound came out. The climax sweeping through her was too intense for her to make a sound. All she could do was grab hold of Clint's arm and the edge of the bunk until the storm within her had passed.

With the feel of her pussy clenching around him and the sight of Lyssa's glistening naked body in front of him, Clint was soon in the grip of that same storm.

TWENTY-FOUR

The sound of boots knocking against the floorboards would have echoed through the cramped confines of the rooms belowdecks if *The Gray Crow* weren't already filled with so many other noises. Between the creaking of the hull, the rush of wind outside and the crash of water against the bottom, most other noises were simply washed away.

It was surprising that the men who'd made those footsteps took a moment to knock, because they simply pushed open the door a second later. Both Clint's and Ernesto's doors were pushed open within a heartbeat of each other.

Ernesto nearly jumped from his bunk, where he'd been sleeping soundly. Although the sailors glaring in at him didn't have their weapons drawn, their hands were on their knives or guns and ready to draw them at the slightest hint of provocation.

Clint wasn't caught quite as off-guard, but he was surprised all the same. By the time his door was opened all the way, the modified Colt was nearly out of its holster.

"Captain wants to see you," the sailor at the head of the bunch said. Glancing back and forth between the two rooms, he added, "All of you. Right away."

"Think we can get a moment to open our eyes?" Lyssa
groused as she made sure enough of her buttons were fas-
tened to keep from giving the sailors a free show.

Although she'd managed to cover herself up, the sailors
still gawked in at her as if she were kicking up her heels on
a stage.

"You look fine just the way you are, darlin'," the same
sailor replied. "Just throw on some shoes and follow us."

Ernesto came out of his room with his shirt buttoned in-
correctly and his pants hanging loosely on his hips. He
tugged on a belt while looking in at Lyssa in much the
same way as the sailors had.

Clint pulled his gun belt around his waist and stepped
into the doorway to give Lyssa a bit of privacy. She only
needed to primp a bit, but Clint was more interested in
making the sailors back off a few steps to give them some
space.

"What's this about?" Clint asked.

Since he couldn't see anything past Clint, the sailor
stopped trying to peek around him. Judging by the angry
look in his eyes, he wasn't too pleased with looking at
Clint rather than Lyssa. "You'll have to ask the captain
about that."

"We made our arrangement and he agreed."

"Yeah," Ernesto said. "We need to rest."

But the sailor wasn't about to be swayed into giving up
any information. In fact, it seemed more apparent that he
truly didn't have much information to give. "Captain's this
way," was all he said.

Once Clint and Ernesto were both in the hall, a few of
the sailors stepped away. Lyssa wasn't far behind. With the
entire group standing out there, it seemed that the cramped
hall was about two seconds away from bursting at the
seams.

"Watch yer step," the sailor said as he pushed open the
door at the front of the hall and stepped through.

Apparently, that one sailor was the only one capable of or interested in speaking. The only noise any of the others made was a few whistles or randy grunts tossed in Lyssa's direction. She took it in stride for the most part, replying only with a few choice grumbles of her own.

Ernesto glanced between her and Clint. Leaning in toward Clint, he whispered, "I was surprised you two were caught with your pants on."

"Really?" Clint asked without even trying to sound interested.

"*Sí.*" Knocking against the closest wood partition he could reach, Ernesto added, "Very thin walls, señor."

Clint rolled his eyes and shrugged. He wasn't even close to being embarrassed by Ernesto's joke. In fact, based on the way all the other men were staring at Lyssa, Clint undoubtedly had some pretty hefty bragging rights in their eyes.

Apart from a few grumbled remarks, nothing much was said as Clint, Lyssa and Ernesto were led through the halls that wound up and down beneath *The Gray Crow*'s decks. In fact, as far as Clint could tell, they'd probably only traveled about thirty feet if it had been in a straight line. As it was, they were forced to navigate through confining halls while ducking under low beams and squeezing through tight doorways.

By the time they reached the door they were after, it seemed as if they'd walked a mile.

"Here you are," the only speaking sailor said. "Captain's just inside." With that, he pushed open the door as if he were a butler showing guests into his master's parlor.

For what seemed to be the fiftieth time in five minutes, Clint ducked his head and stepped over the inch or so of plank that acted as a doorstop. Once all three of them were inside, two of the bulkier sailors stepped in behind them and shut the door.

Captain Layfield was sitting in his chair when they'd arrived. The big man swung his feet down from where they'd been propped and stepped forward to pat all three of them on the shoulders.

"Glad to see you all made it without knocking your heads too many times," Layfield said good-naturedly. "How're your rooms?"

"I guess you get what you pay for," Lyssa said.

Ernesto shrugged. "Can't complain."

"My only complaint is that the doors could use some stronger locks," Clint said.

Layfield shrugged and dropped back down into his seat. "My men are used to hard work and aren't too much for sweet-talking. Hope they didn't barge in on anything too personal." When he said that last part, the captain didn't try to hide the look he plastered onto Lyssa.

"I take it you have some business with us?" Clint asked.

That was enough to bring Layfield back to current matters and peel his eyes from Lyssa's breasts. "I sure do, Adams. Why don't you have a seat?"

With the boat rocking more and more by the second, all three of them were quick to accept that offer.

"Now that you're comfortable," Layfield said, "I want you to know that you're doing a fine job in earning your keep. There's just a few questions I need to ask and if I don't think you're being straight with me, I'll have you tossed off my ship so quickly that you'll be at the bottom before you even know you're wet."

TWENTY-FIVE

Clint had been in plenty of difficult bargaining situations. He knew that a smart man would try to get himself into the best position possible before getting down to business. When it came to Captain Layfield, however, being in a good position was something of an understatement.

Out there, in the ocean and on that creaking boat, there was nowhere to go if things got bad. Clint didn't know exactly where they were, but he was fairly certain they were too far from shore to swim back. He also knew that *The Gray Crow* was filled with plenty of men who would love to get their hands on all three of them for various reasons. None of those reasons were too good.

With all of that becoming painfully clear, there wasn't much else for Clint to do besides say, "Go ahead and ask your questions."

Layfield nodded, knowing full well what had just flashed through Clint's mind. He no longer even regarded the gun around Clint's waist as a threat. He simply looked at the modified Colt as an interesting conversation piece.

"I guess the first thing I should ask is if you truly know what the hell you're gettin' yourself into."

Clint had been expecting plenty of questions from Captain Layfield, but that absolutely wasn't one of them. After thinking it over for a moment, Clint shook his head. "Honestly? No."

A smile cracked Layfield's face and widened as if it were being pulled by two opposing fishhooks caught in his cheeks. "Now that's an honest answer, Clint. Maybe not the smartest, but damn honest."

"I aim to please."

"Well, if you're truly going after Graham Farnsworth, then you'd best aim to stay alive because that's about as good as you can hope for. How's that for honest?"

Lyssa and Ernesto were still looking back and forth at each other as if they didn't know what to think.

After a few offhanded waves from Layfield, the other sailors in the room started backing off. The captain himself was grinning like he was at a party in his honor.

"You probably don't remember me, Adams, but we already met once."

Clint studied the captain's face before snapping his fingers. "San Francisco, right?" When he saw the way Layfield's face lit up, Clint added, "It was at that two-day game of seven-card stud."

"I'll be damned! How the hell do you recall that?"

"Normally, seven-card isn't my game. But staring across all that money at the same bunch of faces for two days tends to burn quite a lot into a man's brain."

Layfield was shaking his head and laughing while he reached under a nearby table. When he pulled his hand back out into the open, it was wrapped around a half-filled bottle sealed with an old cork. "As I recall, you won some money off of me, Adams."

"I won some money off of just about everyone that night, but it all wound up in the pockets of that plantation owner."

"Oh, yeah. That southern son of a bitch."

Lyssa leaned forward so she could catch the eye of the

other two men. "What's going on here?" she asked. "By the way we were pulled from our rooms, I thought there was some sort of trouble. If this was just about catching up on old times, we could have at least been allowed to get dressed in peace."

When the captain looked over to her, the admiration was still plain to see. It was tempered a bit, however, with a subtle touch of respect. "Sorry about that, ma'am, but I needed to have a word with you all so I could know what to make of you. I think we can get along just fine, though, now that I know you're on the up-and-up."

Glancing over to Clint, Lyssa asked, "Is this man serious?"

"I'd say so," Clint replied. "He never was much of a bluffer."

That brought out a laugh from the captain, which boomed throughout the cabin. "Oh Lord, that's something else! Never much of a bluffer! That calls for a drink."

Layfield scrounged up a handful of shot glasses and tossed one to each of the three people in front of him. One by one, he filled Clint's, Lyssa's and Ernesto's glass with the potent contents of the bottle he'd been holding.

"Here's to the start of a good friendship!" Layfield boomed. To Clint, he added, "And here's also to a chance for me to win some of my money back."

Clint never was much for drinking liquor. But when he felt the tension in the air melt away and saw that the other sailors had left them alone, he decided to make an exception.

Lyssa and Ernesto looked a bit confused, but optimistic.

"Bottoms up," Clint said, and then downed the rum he'd been given.

TWENTY-SIX

The Gray Crow pulled up to the dock at Tumbes several days later. Almost immediately, sailors spilled off of the boat to tie it to the dock and set up the gangplank that would carry them off the deck. As soon as the lashed-together planks rattled against the dock, men were stomping over them with cargo on their backs or in their hands.

Tumbes itself was a flurry of activity. At least, the section of docks where *The Gray Crow* had come to rest was covered with locals and merchants like ants swarming over an unattended sandwich. Noise from people and animals alike filled the salty air. Even the sun seemed to have a different shine to it now that its rays were being cast so far south.

After the first preparations had been made and the cargo was being unloaded from the hold, Captain Layfield stomped into the open air and filled his lungs with it. Pounding his chest, he stepped to the edge of his boat and bellowed, "Now, that's a hell of a sight to wake up to!"

Clint and Lyssa came out next. The trip had taken its toll on both of them, but seemed to have been especially hard for Lyssa. Her face was pale in the middle with the slightest hint of green around the edges. Her figure had slimmed down just a bit since she hadn't been able to keep all of her food down throughout the final part of the trip.

Although he'd weathered the storms a little better, Clint was still awfully glad to see dry land. He felt even better when he took a deep breath and got something apart from salt water in the back of his throat for his troubles.

"You smell that, Adams?" Layfield asked. "That there's the smell of Rosie's Cantina and it's the best thing you're likely to smell for the next year or two."

"Maybe I'll try the food there on the way back," Clint said.

"Aw, you're not starting to get squeamish now, are ya? If you didn't toss your guts during that squall the other night, you can handle a nice big bowl of pinto beans dripping with cheese and peppers!"

"Oh, God," Lyssa groaned. "I think I'm going to be sick."

"Speaking of that," Layfield said while glancing over his shoulder at the door leading below the deck, "where's your little friend?"

Ernesto had hated the title he'd been given by the captain. And every time Layfield called him Clint's "little friend," his reaction had been just short of throwing a punch. Ernesto had also been getting twice as sick as Lyssa and for double the time. Because of that, he hardly seemed to care when Layfield shouted back at him with those dreaded words. In fact, it was all Ernesto could do to drag himself out onto the deck without help from one of the other sailors.

"Are we there yet?" Ernesto wheezed. "Can I get off this godforsaken boat?"

"Go on, little friend," Layfield said. "Plank's thataway."

Upon seeing the dock and the land on the other side of it, Ernesto perked up and moved faster than he had in days. He was past Clint and walking into town before anyone else could say another word.

"I really appreciate you bringing us down here," Clint said to the captain. "You're quite a host."

"And you're quite a card player. I swear I had you the other night with that straight. Any other man pulled out a flush on me and I might've knocked him on his ass. But I'll be damned if you're just not that damn lucky, Adams."

"Let's just hope it holds." Clint extended his hand, which was immediately snatched up and shaken by Captain Layfield.

"I'll be staying in port here until you come back," Layfield said. "You've got a job to do, remember?"

"I haven't been thinking about much else."

"Good. If things don't go right, just try to get that bastard Farnsworth close enough to *The Crow* here." With that, Layfield stretched out one leg and kicked what had appeared to be just another stack of cargo roped to the edge of the deck.

Layfield's boot cracked against the side of the pile, causing the burlap cover to fall away. Once that was done, the cannon that was previously hidden was revealed.

Lyssa let out a low whistle. "And all this time Clint was telling me I should stop thinking of this as a pirate ship."

"I don't exactly sail into battle for the hell of it," Layfield said. "But I can hold my own if it comes down to it. Tell you what, Clint. If you can bring Farnsworth close enough for me to point this ol' girl in his direction, then you earned the trip down here and back a couple times over."

"I'll see what I can do," Clint said. "For now, I'd just like to start by trying to find Farnsworth. I've got a sneaking suspicion that another friend of mine won't be too far away."

Layfield dropped a meaty arm across Clint's shoulders and steered him to the edge of the boat. Looking out at the town, Layfield used his other arm to point to where it met up with the jungle. "You see that group of shacks over there?"

Squinting until his eyes had grown accustomed to the light, Clint nodded. "I see them."

"That's where I meet up with Farnsworth when it comes time for him to bend me over and pick my pockets. I would've kicked his ass a while ago if it weren't for all the hired guns he surrounds himself with. Calls them his 'constables.' It's gotten to the point where you say that word to any of the locals and you might as well have mentioned the devil himself."

Clint's eyes roamed over the town of Tumbes. Although it shared plenty of traits with other towns he'd seen, there was something about it that made it plain he wasn't anywhere close to home any longer. It might have been the bright colors worn by the locals or the foreign languages filling the air, but the difference was alive and well.

Even the town itself looked different. Along with the buildings, shacks and tents, there were structures that looked to be as old as the Amazon itself. Hints of gold could be seen in temple walls, although much of it had obviously been chipped out by any number of conquerors who had roamed those lands.

"All right, Adams," Layfield said with another powerful clap on his back. "I'd like to stand around here and shoot the breeze, but I've got work to do."

Clint nodded, fit his hat down tightly onto his head and placed his hand over his holstered Colt. "So do I."

TWENTY-SEVEN

Tumbes, Clint soon realized, was a whole lot more than just another town. It was a city wrapped up in adobe walls which showed wear and tear due to everything from tropical storms to gunfire. The streets were alive with locals wrapped up in colorful shawls and ponchos, with hats that looked strangely formal to the eyes of the Americans.

As they did their best to follow in Ernesto's tracks, Clint and Lyssa nodded to the friendly faces that were turned their way. Of course, for every one of those friendly faces, there were suspicious glares and distrusting sneers coming from beneath the brims of yellow wide-brimmed hats and black bowlers.

"I can see why Danny Miller came down here," Lyssa said.

Clint nodded and smiled up at the bright midday sun. "This place does have a spark in the air. I've heard stories about streets being paved with gold and folks wearing gems in their clothes the way we wear our buttons."

Halfway through all that, Lyssa's eyes had doubled in size. "Really?" she gasped. "Where did you hear about all of this?"

"From some account of an explorer. I think his name was Pizarro. He came through here in the early sixteenth century."

Lyssa's eyes went back to their normal size. In fact, they narrowed down even further into slits, which cut a path straight through to the back of Clint's head. "Very funny." She looked around at the city that now surrounded her. "Still, this place does have something in the air."

"You think this could have something to do with it?" Clint had stopped in front of a wide building with stucco walls. He was pointing up at a sign that had been painted onto the wall in a dark blue. The sign read, ROSIE'S CANTINA.

"Oh yeah," Lyssa said as she stopped and pulled in a deep breath. "That's the smell that will get the blood flowing, all right."

The scents wafting from the cantina were a mix of baking flour and hot peppers. The effect was like having a shot of whiskey dropped into a cup of tea.

"Well, this is where Ernesto went. And if we wait around too much longer, we might just meet up with Captain Layfield again."

"Let's see if we can find Ernesto and get moving. I've had enough of those sailors to last me a while."

All Clint needed to do was step up to the entrance and look in over the bat-wing doors to get a good taste of what was going on inside the cantina. Spotting Ernesto was easy enough, especially since the Mexican was on his way back out through those same doors. Clint took a quick step back to allow the other man to pass.

"We're in luck, señor," Ernesto said in a voice that was still a bit tinged with the sickness that had caused him to spend a good deal of the trip down leaning over *The Gray Crow*'s rail. "Talk of Farnsworth is spreading all over. It seems he and his men looted a small village in the jungle."

"Looted a village?" Lyssa asked, jumping forward like a racing horse at the sound of a gun. "When did that happen?"

"A few days ago. We were either still on land or on that damned boat when it happened."

"Can you take us to the village?" Clint asked.

At first, Ernesto nodded. He then stopped, thought it over and averted his eyes. "I will go back inside and make sure. Wait here."

After Ernesto disappeared into the cantina, Clint pulled in a steady breath and let it out. He felt as if he'd been doused with a quick splash of cold water. He no longer looked around at the scenery or tried to place the exotic smells his nose was finding.

He was there for a specific reason and taking in the sights was not it.

Lyssa, on the other hand, couldn't seem more excited.

"I don't know if Ernesto is the best guide we could have gotten," she said, "but I'll bet he can take us right to where all the action is. We're really going to do this, aren't we, Clint? We're really going to go into that jungle and root out a man who loots villages."

"I'll only tell you this once," Clint said in a tone that was darker than Lyssa had heard from him so far. "If you're out to soak up blood and atmosphere for your story, then you might as well stay right here."

"We're in this together," she replied. "I'm going with you."

"Then you'll go along to help and you'll do what I say. You understand me?"

At first, Lyssa was plainly offended. When she took a moment to think about it, however, she nodded. "You're right. I do want to help, but I am going to write this story."

"I know. Just write it after we're through this. Otherwise, you'll be trying to do too many things at once. With whatever hornet's nest Danny kicked over in that jungle out there, there's plenty for us to worry about."

"Don't worry," Lyssa said earnestly. "We'll watch out for each other."

Ernesto was on his way out. Judging by the look on his face, things were just about to get interesting.

TWENTY-EIGHT

"Are they in there?" Clint asked.

"Farnsworth? No. But the constables already know we are here."

"What? How?"

Ernesto shrugged and shook his head. "*No sé*, but once they heard I was from *The Gray Crow*, it was all they could talk about."

As if to emphasize Ernesto's point, a loud string of words came from inside the cantina. Clint couldn't quite make out what was said, but the words were followed by the smashing of glass against the door frame. Bits of broken bottle and a spray of liquid flew across Ernesto's back.

"I think we should get moving, señor."

"Good idea," Clint said as he took Lyssa by the wrist. "Let's get out of here."

Lyssa struggled against Clint's grasp, but came along with him all the same. By the time they had some space between themselves and the cantina, Clint let go of her.

"I said I'd come with you, Clint," she groused. "No need to pull me around like I'm a child."

"Stay here," was Clint's only reply.

Lyssa took a quick look around and saw that she was

standing just inside an empty nook with a small awning hanging over it. There were plenty of other nooks in that row, but most of them were occupied by a vendor's cart or a small table set up to display any number of wares.

"Are you going to that place Captain Layfield pointed out?" she asked.

"I'll be back for you," Clint said.

"And what if you're not? I mean, what if you can't get back to this spot without trouble?"

"If me or Ernesto don't come back for you in thirty minutes, you get yourself on the other side of the wall surrounding this town and head southeast. Find a spot a little ways in the jungle and stay there. We'll come looking for you."

"How long should I stay there?"

"Until we find you." Clint held her face in his hands and looked straight into her eyes. "You want me to trust you? You'll have to trust me. I won't leave you behind."

Before too long, she nodded. After that, Clint gave her a quick kiss and let her go. Lyssa immediately stepped back and pressed her back against the adobe wall.

"Thirty minutes," Clint said while jogging to catch up with Ernesto.

She checked the clock set into the steeple of a nearby church and crossed her arms. This was going to be a long half hour.

"What, exactly, went on in there?" Clint asked once he'd matched Ernesto's stride.

"Not much. They knew about Layfield's boat arriving at the docks and were saying that I should know better than to sign up with a lying dog like him."

"And how did they know you were with him?"

Ernesto took a sudden interest in one of the shops they were passing and then looked back to Clint with a guilty expression. "I might have said something."

"Jesus. I guess that blows any surprise we might have had."

"I did not know we were going to try and surprise anyone!"

"And I didn't know you'd walk in announcing yourself to the first bunch of drunks you could find."

"The bartender asked where I was from. I was thirsty and said the first thing I could to get a beer."

Clint shook his head. "Next time, try to think before you open your mouth like that or I might start to think you're working for the wrong side."

Ernesto stopped and turned on his heels so he was facing Clint head-on. His hand reached out to snag Clint's sleeve to make sure he wasn't going anywhere just yet.

"You don't trust me?" Ernesto asked.

"You're supposed to be a guide, Ernesto. You wanted to come along with me, so I let you come along. As for me trusting you, that's just something that's going to have to happen along the way.

"For right now, all I can work with is what I can see and what I see is you walk straight into that cantina, tell everyone we're here and that we're looking for Farnsworth. If we switched places, how would you be feeling about me right now?"

There was some anger in Ernesto's eyes, but that faded quickly. "I see what you mean."

"Good," Clint said as he slapped Ernesto on the back. "Now, let's get moving before any of your friends from the cantina decide to look us up."

Although they both got moving at the same time, Clint made sure to keep Ernesto where he could keep an eye on him.

The streets had more twists in them than a sailor's knot, but the building Layfield had pointed out was easy enough to find. Clint knew he was on the right path since it was the same building that Ernesto seemed most anxious to find.

It turned out that the building was on the very edge of town. In fact, the back of it butted right up against the wall surrounding Tumbes. There were no markings on the building, but there were more men standing around outside of it than there had been at the cantina.

Clint still had hopes of getting there before word got around about their arrival. Those hopes were dashed when a skinny kid came running up to the front door amidst a flurry of bony arms and legs.

That kid talked excitedly to the men in front of the place while jabbing his fingers back in the direction of the cantina. When he spotted Ernesto, the kid jumped and started pointing even more furiously.

"Once again, señor," Ernesto grumbled. "I am sorry."

"Save it," Clint replied as he fixed his gaze upon the men who were now headed straight for them. "It was bound to come to this sooner or later."

TWENTY-NINE

"What can I do for you, gentlemen?"

Considering that the question came from the mouth of a dirty man with crooked features, the English accent seemed more than a little out of place. The man stepped forward with his hand resting upon the pistol tucked into his belt.

Two other men who had been standing near the front door of the building were stepping up to stand at the first one's side. Both of them were also armed, with at least two pistols each. At least, those were the weapons that were in plain sight.

Clint stepped right up to within ten feet of the three men, as if he were going to ask them to join him for lunch. A smile adorned his face and he pretended not even to see the guns that were on display.

"I'm looking for an old friend of mine," Clint said. "Maybe you can help me?"

"What's your friend's name?"

"Miller. Danny Miller. He should have come through here about a month or so ago. Maybe he's been around since then?"

"Oh, I think I know that bloke." Turning to one of the

other gunmen nearby, he asked, "Isn't that the bloke we caught sticking his nose into Mister Farnsworth's affairs?"

The other gunman smiled as if he'd just been tickled under the nose. "Yeah. I think so."

The first man turned to look once again at Clint. "Check the jungle. I think we buried him out there."

Clint took another step closer. "This isn't the sort of thing I'd joke about. I've come a long way to find my friend."

"Like I said. Check the jungle. He should still be there unless some animal's dug him up and eaten him by now."

Nodding while he took in the scene in front of him, Clint saw a few more faces staring out from the building. There didn't seem to be any more guns there just yet. "Where's Farnsworth?"

"That's Mister Farnsworth, to you."

"Where is he?"

"Don't worry about that. How about you just march back to your ship and head back home. You're over your head down here. Trust me."

"Is Farnsworth inside?"

The gunman who'd been doing the talking narrowed his eyes into slits. "You deaf? Didn't you hear what I said?"

"Go get Farnsworth, or tell me where he is," Clint snarled. "If you can't do either of those, I don't have much use for you."

The tone in Clint's voice left nothing to the imagination. It also made the first gunman take a closer look at him.

"Get the hell out of here," the gunman said. "Right now."

Clint leaned to one side so he could get a look past the gunmen. There wasn't much to see apart from the front of the building and a few shuttered windows. Just as he was about to look away, one of those shutters came open and a narrow face peered out.

That narrow face was sprouting a generous portion of

gray whiskers. The man's eyes glittered like diamonds in their sockets. In the space of a second, Clint felt that he'd been sized up and evaluated. And when the shutters closed, it was only another two seconds before the owner of those sharp eyes came strutting outside.

"What's going on out here?" the man with the gray whiskers asked.

Clint looked past the gunmen as if they no longer existed. "I'm looking for Mister Farnsworth."

"I'm Graham Farnsworth and this is my place of business. What's the commotion?"

"I think you know a friend of mine. His name's Danny Miller."

Farnsworth's eyes fixed upon Clint for a moment the way a hawk focuses on a mouse. With a similar twitch of his head, he replied, "Never heard of him. Now please leave my property."

"What exactly is your business, Mister Farnsworth?"

The slender gentleman was in the process of turning around. He stopped, snapped one arm out to the side and tapped a small sign that Clint had previously overlooked. "I'm a private surveyor. I assess land interests and acquisitions."

"Do those acquisitions include looting villages?" Clint asked. "Because that's the word that's been going around."

When he'd come up and started talking to these men, Clint's intention had been to see what reaction he would get. At the most, he figured he might ruffle some feathers, but he didn't exactly have time to waste in getting to know what kind of men he was dealing with.

"Is that what you've heard?" Farnsworth asked.

"Yes, sir."

"And I suppose you make a habit of walking up to a man's place of business and throwing out slanderous insults like that?"

"I would have preferred a civilized conversation," Clint

pointed out, "but your boys here don't seem too interested in being civilized."

Farnsworth regarded that for a moment. As he thought it over, his head cocked to one side and the muscles in his jaw tensed beneath his skin. Even though his hands were clasped behind his back, the man's posture and bearing made it easy enough to tell his knuckles were white with the powerful grip he was trying to conceal.

"You're an American," Farnsworth declared. "You know nothing of civilization and you have no right to walk up to me and speak to me in this manner."

"Well, then let me buy you a drink," Clint said. "We can discuss where I might find Danny Miller."

"Mister Miller is no longer a concern and neither are you. I cannot tolerate being treated this way, so I'm afraid we will have to cut this meeting short."

Farnsworth stuck out one arm and leveled it straight at Clint and Ernesto. To his men, he only said two words.

"Kill them."

THIRTY

Clint's first reaction was to try and keep Farnsworth talking. But the Englishman had already turned his back on the outside world after his command had been handed down. The gunmen he left behind appeared to be all too anxious to carry it out.

"I told you to leave," the first gunman said. "Now it's too late."

Taking a few steps back, Clint took a quick look around. As far as he could tell, the only threats in the area were still the three gunmen. There were some others watching from nearby buildings, but the locals already knew only too well to give Farnsworth's building a wide berth.

The first of the gunmen to make a move wasn't the one who'd done all the talking. Instead, the third man in the row made a clumsy grab for the pistol wedged underneath his belt. His hand slapped against the grip, but didn't make it any farther before Clint had drawn his modified Colt and pulled his trigger.

The Colt bucked once in Clint's hand, spitting hot lead toward the first man unfortunate enough to catch his attention.

The gunman in the middle was also the one who'd been the spokesman for the group. He now dropped to one knee, just as the man beside him hit the ground on his back. Gritting his teeth, he plucked one gun from its spot at his waist while attempting to fill his other hand, as well.

Clint reached out with one hand to make sure Ernesto was where he'd left him. When he didn't make contact, he chanced a quick look around to see if his guide was about to stab him in the back.

Although Ernesto wasn't exactly stepping up to defend him, he wasn't trying to make any move against Clint. Instead, he'd dropped to the ground and was rolling to one side. His destination appeared to be a nearby water trough.

Shifting his aim, Clint was about to take his shot when every one of his reflexes screamed out to him. When the lead started to fly, time had a tendency of slowing down a bit. Sound turned into a mush and every second stretched itself out.

In that space between heartbeats, Clint had picked out his targets and taken stock of what Ernesto was doing. All the while, he'd still been on both feet and standing in the open no more than a few paces away from the men now trying to kill him.

One more instant in that spot, and Clint knew he was a dead man.

With no time to do anything fancy, Clint dropped straight down into a squat and pushed himself backward with both legs. As he felt his back roll over the ground, Clint tilted his head to one side to keep from rolling over that as well.

The air over Clint's body exploded as bullets hissed by and smoke bellowed outward. The smell of gunfire caught in Clint's throat and he felt more than saw that he was once again right side up. Clint reached back with one hand while reaching forward with the Colt. From there, he pulled his trigger to send a shot in the general vicinity of the gunmen.

By this time, another burst of gunfire had erupted from

a spot to Clint's left. Reflexively, he twisted at the waist to get a look at its source.

Ernesto's eyes were wide and he was huddled down into almost a quarter of his size. Even with all that, he still managed to draw his gun and take a shot. Chips and dust popped against the trough he was using as cover, causing Ernesto to duck back down behind it.

Clint was still in the open and the bullets were whipping closer and closer to him. After spotting a much better place to be, Clint shuffled in that direction while firing off all his remaining rounds. Even though he wasn't able to aim, his shots made it close enough to send the remaining two gunmen scattering.

That just left the third gunman, who'd been the first one to fall. He was still drawing breath, but he wasn't able to get up and move with the others. Without much say in the matter, he kept as flat as he could while firing at Clint and Ernesto.

Clint wound up with his back pressed against a staircase that led up to a balcony over his head. The stairs were encased in a wooden frame that acted more as a shade than anything else. Luckily, the wood seemed sturdy enough to stop enough rounds to allow Clint a few moments rest.

"How you doing over there, Ernesto?" Clint asked while hurriedly reloading the Colt.

"Almost out of bullets," came the shaky reply.

Clint wasn't too surprised to hear that. Ernesto kept his gun tucked away without wearing it in a holster. That might be good for hiding the weapon, but the price was not having spare ammunition.

Snapping the Colt's cylinder shut, Clint popped a few more bullets from his belt and tossed them toward Ernesto. A few of them bounced into the street, but most of them managed to drop into the trough where Ernesto was hiding.

"Gracias!"

Having done all he could do for Ernesto, Clint chanced a quick look at the gunmen.

The shooting had stopped and one of the gunmen was working his way over to his fallen partner. The spokesman had watched Clint's retreat, which gave him enough confidence to pull himself together and take the offensive.

Sighting down one barrel, the spokesman sent a shot into Ernesto's trough. His other hand was gripping a gun, as well, and he pulled that trigger to send some lead flying in Clint's direction.

Although Clint would have been content to let the gunman waste his ammunition taking offhanded shots, Ernesto's trough didn't look like it was going to stand up to much more punishment. Already, the rectangular box was leaking like a sieve.

Clint caught Ernesto's eye and gave him a nod. He then held up his left hand with fingers extended, retracting each one in a steady countdown. Judging by the way Ernesto made a quick sign of the cross over himself and muttered something to the sky, he knew what Clint had in mind.

THIRTY-ONE

By the time Clint's last finger curled back, both men jumped from their spots and came at the gunmen head-on.

Clint was thinking clearly enough to know that Ernesto probably wouldn't hit much of anything in that charge. But since the other man had pushed away from his leaking trough and was moving at all, Clint considered it a victory. The moment he saw Ernesto bolt from cover, Clint turned his attention to more important matters.

At first, the gunmen were too stunned to do anything. That lasted for a full second before they took stock of what appeared to be two madmen running straight for them. By that time, the lead had started to fly once more and the next part of the fight was on.

Ernesto pulled his trigger again and again, letting out a scream that was swallowed up by the thunder erupting from his fist.

One of the gunmen who'd been about to take a shot shifted his aim toward Ernesto, which was precisely what Clint had been hoping for. Without all the fire coming at him, Clint had some room to maneuver. His first shot punched through the wall just behind the head of the gunman who'd meant to put Ernesto down.

Feeling and hearing that lead whip past him caused the gunman to re-think his intentions and drop down before pulling the trigger.

Ernesto was barely able to see where he was going and had completely missed the fact that Clint had fired. All he saw was the gunman duck and run away in front of him, which gave Ernesto a much-needed jolt of courage. Adding a bit of savagery into his scream, he charged on.

Clint was still running, as well. His eyes had shifted over to the closer gunman, only to find that man taking a shot at him. With all of his senses stretched to their limit, it felt as though Clint were only inches away from the end of the man's barrel when sparks and smoke blasted from it.

It was moments like these that gave a man gray hairs. Clint swore that he felt every speck of dust in the air in the split second it took for his next step to impact against the ground. All that time, he waited to feel hot lead drill through his flesh.

That feeling didn't come at that moment, however. Instead, all Clint felt was a nick, as the bullet narrowly missed him. The round did catch a bit of his side, however, and managed to take some skin and a piece of his shirt along for the ride.

Rather than wait for the gunman in front of him to catch his breath and take better aim, Clint fired his Colt and sent a round into that man's chest.

The impact of the bullet was like a kick from a mule and drove the gunman straight to the ground. He hit the dirt hard and let out a dull grunt. After that, he didn't make another move or utter another sound.

Clint rushed up to the man who had been the first one to take a hit. That gunman was still lying on the ground with his gun in hand. The pistol was smoking, but had become silent now that Clint was standing directly over the man holding it.

"Let it go," Clint said while staring along the top of the

modified Colt. "Unless you want me to finish the job I started."

The wounded gunman glanced at Clint, then down to his hip, which had been the part of him to catch the first bullet Clint had fired in this scuffle. From there, he raised his eyes toward Clint for one more look. When he saw the grim visage staring back down at him, the gunman let out a sigh and let the pistol fall from his grasp.

"Good choice," Clint said.

Ernesto had arrived at the spot he'd been running toward. Now that he was there, he seemed surprised to have made it at all. For a moment, he glanced around with excited confusion. When he caught a glimpse of the last gunman hiding behind a low stucco wall, Ernesto extended his arm rigidly and pointed his gun at him.

There was still some fight in that last gunman's eyes. That spark, however, dwindled away quickly when he saw that nobody else remained to back his play. Slowly, the gunman got to his feet while lifting his arms over his head. When he was standing straight in front of Ernesto, he pitched his gun away.

Ernesto's eyes widened with a mix of shock and glee. For a moment, he couldn't even make a sound. Then, when he caught his breath, he started laughing.

"That's right!" Ernesto said victoriously. "You better give up if you know what's good for you!"

"Ernesto," Clint said. "Just make sure he's not holding any more guns."

"Oh, *sí*."

Clint covered the man on the ground with the gun he'd taken from him while swinging the modified Colt over to aim at Ernesto's prisoner. Ernesto patted the gunman down quickly and stepped back.

"No more guns, señor."

Clint looked back to the front door of the stucco building. As he'd expected, Graham Farnsworth was right there watching over everything.

"You made a big mistake here, Farnsworth," Clint said.

The Englishman nodded and replied, "You're correct about that. Trust me when I tell you I won't be making that same mistake a second time."

"Tell me where to find my friend, and my business here is done."

That brought a humorless smirk to Farnsworth's face. "What was his name? Oh, yes. Danny, was it?"

"That's right."

"Your friend Danny Miller has made plenty of mistakes, himself. His last one was to try to take away something that belongs to me. After that, nobody's seen too much of him."

Farnsworth kept his hands clasped behind his back as he turned and started walking into his building. Glancing over his shoulder, he said, "What you've done here today is a bigger mistake than Mister Miller could ever dream of committing. Think about that in what little time you have left."

With that, Farnsworth disappeared into the building and shut the door behind him.

"Maybe we should go now," Ernesto said.

Looking around, Clint saw dozens of eyes glaring down at him from the windows overlooking the street. Most of those eyes were also sighting down rifle barrels.

"Yeah," Clint said. "That sounds like a good idea."

THIRTY-TWO

Clint could feel those eyes staring down at him from every angle. It was a sensation that crept along the back of his neck and sent a chill through him that stood in stark contrast to the muggy heat hanging in the air.

It seemed that Farnsworth had riflemen perched in enough places that at least two of them could put a bullet into any spot within eyeshot of the Englishman's building. Clint backed away and eased his Colt back into its holster, signaling for Ernesto to do the same.

The fire that Ernesto had been feeling before was now nowhere to be found. Instead, he was glancing back fondly to his spot behind the leaking trough.

"What should we do, señor?"

"Don't make any sudden moves," Clint said. "We'll just head back the way we came."

Although he wasn't much for turning his back to those guns, Clint figured there already were plenty of guns aimed at his back, anyway. The farther he and Ernesto got from Farnsworth, however, the more of those guns disappeared into the shadows.

Even so, Clint wasn't about to let his guard down anytime soon.

Ernesto let out another sigh. "That was close. I'm glad it's over."

"Yeah. Real close."

"I never thought I had it in me to do anything like that."

Clint nodded at the few words he'd actually heard. "Captain Layfield unloaded the horses and put them into the stalls by the dock. Why don't you go over there and get them?"

"*Sí, sí.* Should I bring them back here?"

"No. Do you know where Danny was headed after he made it here?"

Ernesto nodded. "He was headed into the jungle. I didn't go with him, but I did tell him which way to go to get to where he was going."

"And where, exactly, was that?"

"To an Incan temple just off a basin of the Amazon."

"If we were headed there from here, which way would we go?" Clint asked.

"There's a road leading south out of town," Ernesto replied without hesitation. "We would take that road into the jungle and—"

"That's where I want you to meet us," Clint interrupted. "Get the horses and head out that way. Take your time and we'll catch up with you."

"You and Lyssa?"

"Yep. You didn't think I'd leave her now that we made it this far, did you?"

Ernesto looked around as if he expected the reporter to be watching them from the shadows like all of the riflemen surrounding Farnsworth's place. "I think it might not be a bad idea. She could still get herself and the rest of us hurt. Maybe worse."

"You know," Clint said as he leaned over to Ernesto, "the same thing might be said about me taking you along."

Ernesto's eyes widened with genuine offense. "I handle myself pretty well, señor! Didn't you see?"

"Oh, I saw plenty."

"And I still know my way around this jungle. I grew up here, after all."

"You did?"

"*Sí,*" Ernesto said as he straightened up proudly. "Just because I didn't say before, that doesn't mean it's not so. It's been a while since I've been here, but I should be able to find enough familiar faces to show us the way."

"No need to convince me," Clint said. "I don't have a problem with you yet. I also don't have a problem with Lyssa just yet, so we're not ditching her here."

After a moment of thinking it over, Ernesto shrugged and said, "I'll get the horses."

"I appreciate that."

Still grumbling to himself, Ernesto broke away from Clint and walked down a street that branched toward the docks. He was swallowed up quickly by the crowds of Tumbes which flowed normally once again now that Farnsworth was nowhere to be seen.

Clint could see the marketplace where he'd left Lyssa. Unfortunately, he didn't see the fist rushing toward him until it knocked him square in the jaw.

THIRTY-THREE

Staggering to one side, Clint felt as if someone had picked up the ground and was shaking it like a carpet beneath his feet. The pain from the punch filled his entire skull and the sound of it still echoed through his ears.

Working on instinct more than anything else, Clint twisted on the balls of his feet toward the source of the punch. He came face to face with a burly man bearing the features and skin tone of most of the other locals. His wide face bore an even wider smile and his dark eyes were narrowed into cruel slits.

"Señor Farnsworth sends his best," the man said in a scratchy voice. As if to punctuate his message, the man cocked back his fist and prepared to sent it right down Clint's throat.

Clint was still wobbly on his feet, but that only helped him as he bent both knees and curled himself into a tight crouch. The dizziness was fading a bit, but got Clint staggering away from his attacker. When he regained his bearing, Clint found himself backed against a wall. From there, he had only one place to go.

Clenching both fists, Clint brought his arms together and swung them forward as if he were taking a swing with

132

an axe. Both fists connected against his attacker's stomach, doubling the other man over while driving all the wind from his lungs.

But Clint didn't have much time to celebrate. With the first attacker on his way down, another one could be seen rushing forward with a gun already drawn.

Clint grabbed hold of the first man by his shirt collar and yanked him back into a standing position. He then pressed the bottom of his boot against the man's hip and pushed him forward. One attacker bounced against the other, giving Clint just enough room to catch his breath.

The first attacker was still reeling from getting the tables so suddenly turned on him. As Clint rushed by, he sent a quick backhand to that man's temple. The impact was strong and crisp, bringing the bigger man to one knee.

From there, Clint swung his other hand outward to smack against the second attacker's wrist. Upon impact, the man holding the gun pulled the trigger. That was a reflexive twitch, however, and sent a bullet into the closest wall.

Clint sent one jab into the gunman's stomach, following up with a strong uppercut, which landed on the man's chin.

Now that he was a bit closer, Clint could see that these men were perfectly cut out for a hand-to-hand fight. They were thick-skinned and toughened from a life in the harsh embrace of the Amazon. Although Clint had landed his share of punches, both attackers seemed to be recovering from them quickly.

As the first man got back up, the second one was shaking off the effect of Clint's blow. Before he could get his wits completely about him, the man felt a sharp jolt of pain against his right wrist.

Clint had flattened his hand out and sent it into that wrist. He didn't hear any bones break, but he did see the gun drop from the man's grasp. The moment the pistol hit the ground, Clint kicked it away with a sweeping boot.

The pistol spun against the packed dirt and skidded toward the street. before it got there, it was stopped by another boot. Unlike the one that had sent the gun on its way, this boot was made from the skins of snakes pulled from the surrounding jungle.

Reaching down, the owner of those snakeskin boots swept up the gun and draped his finger over its trigger. His other hand came up as well and was wrapped around the pistol that he'd drawn from his own holster. With a gun in each hand, the man set his sights on Clint and walked forward.

Clint wasn't able to keep track of the gun he'd kicked away. He was barely able to keep track of the fists, knees and elbows that were raining down on him in a continuous storm. Although he was able to keep himself from getting hurt by the onslaught, Clint didn't have a chance to do much else.

Finally, he felt his senses start to fade as one blow after another built up and started to take their toll. Clint knew he could either let himself drown under all that punishment or rise above it. The choice was an easy one to make.

Gritting his teeth, Clint lashed out with one fist and then another. He couldn't tell where his punches would land, but he knew he would definitely hit someone with one or both of them. Sure enough, his knuckles slammed against another body.

A curse in Spanish sliced through the air as both attackers backed up a step.

That was all Clint needed to swing the momentum back in his direction. By the looks of it, he'd managed to stun the attacker who'd been the first one to jump him. Clint sent one knee into that man's gut and was glad to hear the rush of air come out of the man's mouth.

Just then, the second attacker took a swing at him, but Clint was able to duck beneath it and deliver one of his own. Clint's fist hooked up and slammed into the other man's stomach. This time, however, it felt as if Clint had tried to punch a brick wall.

Clint might not have done any damage, but he bought himself just enough time to cock his right arm back and send it out again with every bit of his strength behind it. His fist connected with a jarring crack and snapped the other man's head back.

Clint knew that still wouldn't be enough to put the man down. What closed the deal was when the back of the man's head bounced against a wall.

The other man's mouth hung open and he tried to lift his fists. He got them raised about halfway before his eyes rolled up and he collapsed in a heap on the ground.

Clint turned on his heels and started to move in the direction he'd originally been headed. That was when he came face-to-face with the man holding a gun in each hand and wearing snakeskin boots on his feet.

"*Adios*, señor," was all the two-gun shooter said before tightening his grip on both triggers.

There was a sound that echoed through the air, but it wasn't exactly the one Clint had been expecting. Instead of gunfire, it was the sound of iron banging against something almost as hard.

The two-gun shooter was still smiling, but he was also wobbling on his feet. Soon, his expression became vacant and he fell over to one side.

Once the shooter was down, Clint could see Lyssa standing behind him. Her hands were wrapped around the handle of a skillet, which she still brandished as her only weapon.

"What the hell are you doing?" Clint asked.

Lyssa blinked a few times and took a few quick breaths. Once she took in the scene around her, she replied, "Looks like I'm saving your hide, Clint Adams."

At that moment, Clint wasn't able to disagree. But rather than swap banter with the reporter while the other men pulled themselves together, Clint ran forward and took hold of Lyssa's arm.

"How did you find me?" Clint asked.

"Are you kidding? I was following the sound of shooting when you went and got yourself into another fight."

"Come on," he said while pulling her away. "If we don't leave quickly, it'll take a whole cupboard of pots and pans to get us out of here in one piece."

Lyssa was more than happy to oblige.

THIRTY-FOUR

Clint was never the sort to run away with his tail tucked between his legs. When he left Tumbes, he did so without giving Farnsworth or his men enough time to line up another ambush. As he and Lyssa made their way to the road leading out of town, they were given plenty of admiring nods from the locals.

None of the residents or business owners had stepped in on Clint's behalf, but it was clear that none of them had lent a hand to Farnsworth, either. Clint returned those admiring nods with a few friendly waves of his own. The smiles he got from that gave him plenty of hope for getting back into Tumbes without Farnsworth immediately being tipped off.

After all was said and done, Clint and Lyssa were holding their heads high as they stepped beyond the wall surrounding Tumbes. Considering how many of Farnsworth's hired guns they'd needed to get through to get to that spot, Clint wasn't about to keep pushing his luck by sticking around. Once they were on the other side of that wall, they kept right on walking.

"Aren't we forgetting someone?" Lyssa asked. "Actually, aren't we forgetting someone and a few horses, as well?"

Clint had already reloaded the Colt, but had yet to take his hand from the pistol's grip. His face was just about to become as concerned as Lyssa's when suddenly he said, "I think we just found the answer to that question."

Lyssa followed Clint's stare and spotted several figures stepping out of the trees surrounding the path. One of those figures was made to look even smaller by the horses that surrounded him. Ernesto walked out to meet them wearing a wide smile.

"*Hola,* amigos!" Ernesto shouted.

"Did anyone spot you with the horses?" Clint asked.

"Does it matter? When I get them, I hear everyone talking about the shots being fired by Señor Farnsworth. Nothing goes on in these parts without him knowing about it."

"True enough, but that doesn't mean we should make it easy for him to follow us."

Ernesto winked and climbed into his saddle. "Once we get into the jungle, nothing will be easy. Following us . . . that will be almost impossible.

Lyssa had climbed onto her horse as Clint was taking a moment to look over Eclipse. The Darley Arabian seemed a little rattled by the drastic change in scenery, but was more than ready to explore. Clint patted the stallion's neck and then lifted himself into the saddle.

"We take this trail south for a few miles until it forks," Ernesto said. "We can ride until then, but after that we may need to walk."

"Lead the way," Clint said. "As we ride, you can tell me all you know about Farnsworth and what connection he has to Danny."

The three of them were moving at a steady walk, surrounded on all sides by the thick tangle of trees and the leafy canopy of the Amazon jungle. The air was heavy with so many different scents that it formed a soup in the backs of their noses and throats. Birds and insects all screamed at each other from thousands of perches on every side.

Everywhere Clint looked, he saw something moving. Whether it was a snake hanging from a tree limb, a beetle scurrying under a log or a lizard jumping down from a trunk, he couldn't find one spot that was content with sitting still.

As Lyssa looked around, she shrank more and more into her saddle. She also steered her spotted mare so close to Eclipse's side that she almost tripped the Darley Arabian.

Ernesto, on the other hand, looked more comfortable than he had since Clint had first laid eyes on him. Sitting relaxed upon his horse, he guided the animal with casual ease and didn't even flinch as things on either side of him hissed, squawked or spat in his direction.

"I can tell you what I know about your friend Danny," Ernesto said. "Not much, señor. That's what I know."

"Great. That helps a lot."

Ernesto held up a finger and said, "But I do know where he was headed. He was very excited about coming here and couldn't stop talking about all the riches he would find when he brought in our mutual friend, Mister Farnsworth."

"Didn't look like he made much of a dent there," Clint said with a shake of his head.

"Sí. He bites more than he chews, I think. I told him to look up a man I know down here by the name of Topac."

"Topac? Is he a friend of yours?"

"A business associate, perhaps." When he said those words, they seemed uncomfortable in Ernesto's mouth. Grimacing, he added, "We pass word about one another whenever we can. I used to live in Brazil and traveled here every now and then. Once I come to America, I don't get the chance to talk to my partners back home."

"Is this man still where you left him?" Clint asked. "Folks tend to move around a lot, you know."

"Folks where you live move around a lot. Around here, it is healthier to know your home like the back of your hand and then stay there."

Looking around at the jungle and feeling it nip at him from practically every angle, Clint had no trouble believing what Ernesto was saying. By the looks of it, a man's home in that part of the world changed enough on its own without him having to pull up stakes and move to a new spot.

"And what kind of business was this Topac in?" Clint asked.

"Mostly trading. Plenty of business flows up and down the Amazon River. Sometimes, that river twists and turns so much it can swallow up someone who doesn't know their way. Topac knows all the ways in, out and through that river. This is why your friend Danny wanted to talk to him."

"And you told him where to find Topac?"

"*Sí.*"

"How long until we get there?"

Ernesto glanced up the path a ways and then did some figuring in his head. When he was done, he looked over to Clint and said, "I will know the village when I see it."

For some reason, that didn't inspire too much confidence in Clint's mind.

THIRTY-FIVE

They rode for a full day. In the jungle, however, that day felt more like a week.

Compared to the riding Clint was used to, this was more like trudging through molasses while wearing a dozen horse blankets strapped to his back. The air got thicker and hotter with every step. He could have removed his shirt or hat if he didn't mind the possibility of getting scratched by branches or eaten alive by insects.

What made the journey even better was when they woke up from their three hours of sleep to find they could no longer ride their horses. The canopy of tree branches was hanging so low that one or all of them would have wound up snarled up and hung in them unless they dropped down from their saddles to lead the horses by the reins.

Ernesto took the lead and started hacking away at the branches with a machete he'd purchased before leaving Tumbes. More than once, the path they were on simply ended at a pile of fallen trees, a rock wall or an animal's den. By this time, Clint had gotten a handle on his sense of direction. He knew at least enough to tell that they weren't being led in circles.

In the scheme of things, that was enough to keep Clint's

mind busy while the rest of him was swatting mosquitoes or stepping over the snakes that hissed at him on all sides.

Lyssa was quieter than she'd been since Clint had met her. Throughout the entire trek through the jungle, she never said more than two words, and those only came when someone spoke to her first. Clint was about to chalk that up to her being nervous in the strange surroundings, but that opinion changed when he saw what she was doing.

Any chance she could, Lyssa was scribbling on a folded piece of paper. She never stopped writing unless it was absolutely necessary and when she occasionally looked over at Clint, she started writing even more furiously.

Clint wasn't about to snoop at what she was writing, so he simply enjoyed the reprieve from her constant badgering for an interview. Of course, he guessed that opinion would change when he got a look at the story that she was working on.

It was late in the afternoon when Ernesto signaled for the group to come to a stop. His arm was raised slightly and cocked back, holding the machete over his head in preparation for a swing. He let out a quick *shush*ing sound, which caused even the horses to stop out of reflex.

After a few moments, Clint asked, "What is it?"

Ernesto's eyes were darting back and forth. Slowly, he turned his head to get a look back at Clint. "I think we are close to the village."

Taking a moment to study the path ahead of them, Clint stared at the overgrowth. "Are you sure?"

"We should be here, but that smell makes me think there's trouble."

"Smell? What smell?" The truth of the matter was that Clint's nose had been bombarded with so many smells they no longer made any sense. It was like a soup that had too many different spices in it. Before too long, it all turned into a tasteless mush.

"Come here and see for yourself."

Although Ernesto was only a few paces in front of him, Clint decided to humor him and walk up to where he was standing. Sure enough, when he got there, Clint did pick up a different scent in the air.

Pulling in another few sniffs, Clint said, "Smells like something's burning." At the very thought of that, Clint felt his hackles raise. When he looked around, however, he didn't see any flames, smoke or even blackened remains of where a fire might have been.

Ernesto nodded. "That is never a good thing, señor. Not with so many trees around."

"I see what you mean, but the smell isn't that strong."

"*Sí*. I think maybe a few days old." He filled his lungs again and added, "Maybe longer."

"And the village is that direction?"

"*Sí*."

"Then let's keep moving."

After a rush of footsteps, Lyssa was standing directly behind them. "Village? Did you say we're almost at the village?"

"Yeah," Clint replied. "Or at least whatever is left of it."

THIRTY-SIX

Ernesto took one last swipe with the machete and made an opening into empty space. A clump of branches fell away to join the rest of the mulch underfoot, revealing a clearing filled with several shacks, tents and lean-tos.

The smell that they'd caught earlier was overpowering at first, much like a plume of dust which had been trapped in a cellar for too long. After that first wave of odor washed over them, the three travelers stepped through the opening and into the village's perimeter.

Clint wiped at his nose as if he could wipe away the stench of charred wood and burnt leaves. All he managed to do was rub in the ash that they'd kicked up upon their arrival. With those few swipes of his hand against his face, Clint felt the grimy cinders smearing into his skin.

Lyssa walked forward and immediately started hacking uncontrollably. Ernesto wasn't too pleased with the scent, either, but managed to force back his own coughs by pulling up the bandanna from around his neck and onto the edge of his nose.

"Is this the place you meant to take us?" Lyssa asked.

Ernesto looked around and walked a few more paces forward. Before too long, he started nodding. *"Sí,"* he said in a voice that was muffled by the bandanna over his mouth. "This is the place, but . . ."

"But it wasn't like this when you left it," Clint said, finishing where the other man had left off.

Clint walked forward, as well. He was holding the reins for Eclipse as well as Ernesto's horse and both animals followed him reluctantly into the village. It was obvious that they were as nervous in the village as the rest of the group. After being surrounded by so much life, being dropped into a burned-out pit was a jolt to their systems.

When he got to the first row of shacks, Clint reached out and touched one of the frames. The blackened wood flaked off and turned to dust in his fingers. Walking around to the front of the shacks, he saw that only a quarter of the frames were still standing and that was mostly due to random luck.

"This happened a while ago," Clint said. "By the looks of it, there must have been at least three or four good rains dousing this place since the fire happened."

Ernesto let out a short laugh. "That could have happened in a few days, señor."

"Maybe, but the folks who lived here haven't been gone for more than a week or two."

Lyssa stepped up beside Clint. Her eyes drank in everything around her. "How can you tell?"

Clint pointed into one of the shacks. "There're still some belongings laying on the floor in there. It looks wet, but there's no moss or mold on any of it, so it hasn't been there long. And it looks like the entire place was practically burned to the ground. If it was too fresh, I'd think there would still be plenty of smoke trapped under all these trees."

Lyssa glanced overhead to see that most of the sky was indeed blotted out by the jungle's natural roof. A few wisps of smoke curled up there, like snakes dancing on the stirring breeze.

The village was in the basic shape of a circle with

everything radiating from a central clearing like spokes from the hub of a wheel. None of the shacks was big enough to have more than one room in them and the tents weren't much smaller.

Although not many of the structures were standing, it was easy enough to pick out where more had been by the square piles of rubble and ash situated next to some of the more fortunate ones. There were signs that people had lived there, such as hitching posts and cooking pits, but that only served to make the village seem all the more empty.

"What do you think, Ernesto?" Clint asked.

"I am no tracker, but I would agree with you. I was looking more at the trees around the edge of the village. How come they are not burned as well? Most fires I hear about come from the trees or spread in that direction. These here are hardly touched."

Clint looked around and quickly found truth in Ernesto's words. From where he was standing, Clint could make out most of the small village's perimeter. Although some of the trees there were dark husks, most of them had taken very little or no damage.

Walking to the center of the empty village, Clint held his hands up to frame a spot that was blackened right down to the dirt under his feet. "If I had to guess, I'd say this is where it started."

Suddenly, there came the sound of a metallic click followed by a scratchy voice. A figure took half a step out from one of the partially standing shacks. "And unless you get your asses out of here," the man said as he stared at Clint and Ernesto over the barrel of his rifle, "this is where it'll end."

THIRTY-SEVEN

Clint heard the round being levered into the rifle's chamber. He heard the crunch of boots against ash and rubble. There was no question that he heard the threat tossed at him in that gravelly voice. At that moment, after all he'd been through, he was almost too tired to care.

"Come on out of there," Clint said. "We're not here to hurt anyone."

The figure standing in what remained of a doorway didn't move. Then, his head cocked slightly to one side. "How do I know that?"

Clint shook his head and started walking straight toward the shack. When he started laughing, it surprised Ernesto and Lyssa more than the shadowy figure holding the rifle.

"What do you think we're going to do?" Clint asked. "Burn the place down?"

"I just . . ." the figure stammered. "You should . . ."

"Come on, Danny. We came too far through this damn jungle to play games with you."

Lyssa's eyes snapped wide open. "Danny? Is that Danny Miller?"

Even Ernesto was leaning forward to get a better look at the figure standing in the shadows. It seemed as though everyone else had forgotten about the rifle in the man's hands.

The rifle's barrel wavered slightly as the man holding it took a few steps out into the light. The man holding it was as dirty as the rest of the village. His clothes were blackened by ash. The skin of his arms, neck and face was smeared with it. It seemed that the only place on him not covered in black or gray was his teeth, which he now bared in a wide smile.

"Clint?" the man said. "Is that really you?"

Clint was already stepping forward. "In the flesh."

Danny Miller lowered the rifle and set it down, freeing up both arms so he could rush forward and wrap them around Clint. "I'll be damned! It really is you!"

When he could catch his breath, Clint got free of Danny's embrace and dusted off the ash that had been left behind.

"Oh, sorry about that," Danny said. "What are you doing here?" As if noticing the others for the first time, he added, "And who's this with you? Wait a second! Is that Ernesto?"

Nodding, Ernesto stepped back in expectation of getting embraced as well and simply said, *"Sí."*

"Can't say as I recognize the lady."

Lyssa rushed forward before anyone else could say a word. She was holding her hand out and practically tripping over herself to speak to the dirty man with the beaming smile. "I'm Lyssa Olam, a reporter for a well-known newspaper circulated throughout the country," she recited.

Danny did a passable job of looking interested in what she said as he drank in the sight of her coming straight for him. "Pleased to meet you, Lyssa."

"I'd love to have a moment to ask you some—"

"There'll be time for that later," Clint interrupted. "First of all, I've got some questions of my own. What the hell happened here?"

That snapped Danny out of his daydreams and wiped the smile from his face. "Man by the name of Graham Farnsworth came through here and burned it down."

"We've met up with Farnsworth."

"Then I suppose you had to pay taxes? Nobody gets away from him without either handing over everything they own or handing over their life."

"It was close, but we didn't hand over any taxes."

Danny's smile returned as he nodded and said, "That's what I like about you, Clint. Never take any shit from no-body."

Ignoring the good-natured slap on his shoulder, Clint said, "The next thing I want to know is what the hell you're doing here."

"I came down here looking to bring in Farnsworth. He's, uh, wanted back in the U.S."

"No need to put a story together," Clint said. "I heard about the treasure."

"Yeah? Well I suppose that doesn't matter, anyway. Farnsworth was supposed to know something about some Inca gold or some such, but I haven't been able to get a damn word out of him or his men."

"And when did you ask him?" Lyssa asked.

"Yeah," Clint said. "Was that before or after he torched this village?"

Danny shook his head and wandered out of the shack. Standing out in the open, he seemed even dirtier than before. When he got to a pile of wood that looked sturdy enough, he lowered himself down to sit on it. He ran his fingers through his short hair, which set a black cloud moving around him.

"Bringing Farnsworth in was supposed to be a big enough job for me to quit this business once and for all," Danny said. "I tracked him all the way down through Mexico and the closer I got, the more I started hearing about this gold he was after.

"That came from one of his men. I tracked that son of a bitch all the way back up through California and then down again before I heard that Farnsworth himself had already gotten himself set up down here. All that work chasing that bastard and I wind up here."

Clint lowered himself down to sit next to Danny. "That still doesn't explain this place," he said.

Danny shook his head while looking around at the remains of the village. "I got down here and thought Farnsworth would be easy enough to find. Hell, when he came over from England, he wasn't much more than an errand boy for some cattle barons. I lost track of him for a while and now he's practically running this place. Well, the civilized parts, anyway."

Lyssa sat down on Danny's other side. There wasn't much room to spare on that woodpile, but she managed to perch herself on what little space there was. "How long have you been after Farnsworth?"

"Damn near a year or so." He closed his eyes and grumbled, "Jesus, it's closer to two, by now."

"Two years?"

Danny nodded. "Time slips past me when I get on a man's trail. Farnsworth pissed off some rich men, so the price on his head was bigger than I'd ever seen. It wasn't exactly legal, but big enough to buy my family a nice piece of land somewhere and some cattle of our own."

"That's sweet," Lyssa purred. "A bounty hunter fighting to give his family a better life."

"Yeah," Clint grunted. "Real sweet. Why don't you ask him how he intended to make their lives so great by doing illegal jobs for bloodthirsty cattle barons?"

"Aw, Clint, it's not like that," Danny groaned. "I just got carried away. And after wasting so much time on this job, I couldn't just let it go for nothing. When I heard about the gold, I saw it as a sign. Even if I split some of that with whoever helped me find it, I would still be able to settle down. I've seen gold miners buy their own ranches with a smaller haul than that."

"So you decided to take a rest from chasing down your fortune by camping in a burned-out village?" Clint asked.

Danny let out an exasperated breath. "When I came down here, I thought I was after the same Farnsworth that I'd been chasing from the start. But he's not that man anymore, Clint. He's got himself set up here like he's been here for years. He's got himself surrounded with hired guns, he's got at least two or three businesses set up in towns all through the country and he's even got a piece of the shipping trade. I just don't see how I could have misjudged him so badly."

"Maybe you haven't misjudged him," Clint pointed out. "Maybe our friend Farnsworth has just come into a bit of money and has invested in his own future."

"A bit of money?" Danny asked warily.

"Yeah. Like maybe an inheritance or . . . I don't know . . . a fortune in Incan gold."

THIRTY-EIGHT

Danny's mouth was hanging down as if he simply didn't have the strength to keep it shut any longer. When Clint looked around at the others, he found similar expressions upon Lyssa's and Ernesto's faces.

"What?" the three asked Clint in unison.

Clint shrugged. "Doesn't it make sense? I mean, with all these people out to find this treasure, why is it so unreasonable to think that someone would have found it?"

"But you said there might not even be a treasure!" Lyssa pointed out.

"I could have been wrong. You thought there was a treasure." Glancing over to Ernesto and Danny, Clint pointed to each one in turn and said, "So did the two of you. Personally, I don't believe in wasting your life scrounging for treasure, but that doesn't mean that there's none to be found."

"I don't believe this," Danny said. He'd smacked the heel of his hand against his forehead and was now pressing it there. Every now and then, he twisted his hand as though he was grinding out a cigarette. "This is awful."

"Hold on," Ernesto said. "You mean the treasure's gone? How could that be? How do you know this?"

"I don't know for certain," Clint explained, "but it all fits. Danny here was chasing Farnsworth long enough to know he was a man doing dirty work for other men higher up than him on the chain. Is that right?"

Danny nodded.

"And since I know Danny well enough to know how stubborn he is, I believe him on that account. He may be a lot of things, but he's still a hell of a bounty hunter."

"Thanks, Clint."

"That wasn't exactly a compliment," Clint said dryly. "Anyway, he hears about this gold from Farnsworth and then loses track of him a while after. Am I still on the right trail?"

Slumping down and grinding both hands against his forehead, Danny nodded as if the very motion of it caused him pain.

"It takes a while, but Danny finally catches wind of where Farnsworth wound up. When he gets here, he finds Farnsworth to be a man of power, an owner of property and the boss of plenty of bad men of his own."

Clint looked over to Danny. For the first time since he'd ever crossed paths with him, Clint actually felt sorry for the bounty hunter. He'd seen Danny take on more than he could handle. He'd seen Danny charge in where he had no business going. But he'd never seen Danny look so completely and utterly defeated.

"You got stuck here, didn't you?" Clint asked.

Although it hadn't seemed possible, Danny actually slumped a little further down. "Yeah," he groaned. "None of the guides I hired would take me any further than this village. I went out on my own and soon I found that the whole damn jungle was rigged."

"Rigged?" Clint asked. "What's that supposed to mean?"

"You know, traps. There were hunting snares, pit traps, you name it."

Clint looked over to Ernesto and asked, "Did you see any of that when we were coming here?"

Ernesto shrugged. "There are always some traps set up to keep animals away or catch them for food. I guess there were a few more than usual, but I took care of them."

"Well, it would have been nice to have him along when I was trying to cut through that shit," Danny muttered. "I got hung up a few times even before Farnsworth started coming after me. Once he got wind that I was still around, he started trying to flush me out by sending his guns my way and burning down every damn place I stopped.

"I was lucky to find my way back here for some rest and supplies and when I did, it was burned to the ground! I might be able to find my way back to Tumbes, but Farnsworth practically owns that town." He stopped there for a moment and smacked himself on the head. "I can't believe I didn't see that he already found that gold. How stupid can I be?"

"Not stupid," Lyssa said as she wrapped her arm around him and rubbed his shoulder consolingly. "You just didn't want to see it."

"What about the law?" Clint asked. "I know it's not the same down here, but there's got to be someone standing in the way of Farnsworth just doing what he pleases."

"Farnsworth gets free reign. I've asked every local I could find and they all say the same thing. What keeps him in business is the guns he's hired and the taxes he collects. As long as folks pay the taxes, they stay healthy. Actually, Farnsworth takes care of the folks who pay him. It's not a bad deal, if you can afford it."

"Yeah, or if you don't mind being under someone's thumb," Clint said. "Do you want to get out of here or not, Danny?"

"Hell, yes, I want to get out! It's just that there's nowhere for me to go and nobody crazy enough to let me onto a boat or train or even a coach if I can pick my way out of this goddamn jungle."

"Well, I've got a man who's willing to take you out of here."

Danny's eyes brightened. "Really?"

"Really."

"Why go through all this trouble for me, Clint? I mean, I appreciate it and all, but . . . damn . . . you came all the way into this godforsaken jungle for me? I've never been anything but trouble for you."

"That's true. But this is the last time. When I drag your sorry carcass back to your family, I won't be doing it again. Unless you know anyone else as patient as me, you've used up your final reprieve."

"I've been saying it to myself every hour I've been stuck in this hellhole and now I'll say it to you." Danny looked Clint dead in the eyes and vowed, "If I get out of this mess, I'll be a new man. I'm done with chasing bounties. I just want to get a patch of land and raise some pigs."

Clint smirked. "You want to raise pigs?"

Danny smirked as well, but his was tired. It was tired right down to the bone. "I know that sounds silly, but I think that's something I could manage. The main thing would be that I'd be close to my family once again. You've got to believe me, Clint. I'm done with this damn job."

Getting to his feet, Clint said, "I believe you, Danny. If you were lying, you'd come up with something a hell of a lot better than raising pigs. Let's get out of here."

THIRTY-NINE

For a man who'd spent his whole life in the jungles of the Amazon, the chatter of birds and calls of animals faded away into the scenery. It was a quiet life, which was just the way the locals preferred it. After all, there were enough things in the jungle to worry about besides the wildlife.

One of those things caught Topac's attention as he was making his rounds from one hut to the other.

Topac never rallied support to be the leader of his people. The mantle of power had been slowly lowered onto his shoulders after years of tending to their needs and listening to their voices. At first, Topac hadn't been happy with his new responsibilities. But he soon grew accustomed to wearing that mantle and took it very seriously.

Like one of the animals in the jungle protecting its den, Topac stopped what he was doing and turned his sharp eyes to the surrounding trees. After the last week or so, he'd spent more and more time walking the perimeter of his villages. That was where the trouble always started.

"Who's there?" Topac asked in English, which was the language used by the greatest predator of them all.

Like the other times trouble had stepped in from the trees, a man walked into the village surrounded by a few others. Unlike the times when Farnsworth had paid him a visit, these new arrivals used one of the beaten paths leading into the village.

"Howdy, Topac," Danny said while holding both hands up high for the other man to see.

Topac's eyes narrowed as he took in the sight of Danny Miller and the others with him. "I told you before, Señor Miller. I will not help you plunder the gold of my ancestors."

Danny grimaced at the sound of that. He shot a cringing look back to Clint. "I uh, I'm not after that gold anymore."

"Then why are you here? And who is that with you?"

"These are some friends of mine," Danny explained. "They're here to help me get back to where I belong."

Topac gave Danny an abrupt nod. "You belong far away from here. Some of my people even say you are the bearer of bad fortune."

"I'm not about to argue that," Clint said as he took a step forward. "I was just hoping to have a word with you about something that concerns you and your people."

"Who are you?" Topac asked suspiciously.

"My name's Clint Adams."

"Well, Clint Adams, Tumbes is north of here. You should be able to find a boat back to your country there. I would offer you more hospitality, but my people and I grow weary of men stomping through here wearing guns."

"Actually," Clint said, "that's exactly what I wanted to talk to you about."

Topac's expression shifted subtly. It wasn't much, but his interest did seem to be perked. "Go on."

"I hear a man named Farnsworth has been making some trouble for just about everyone around here."

Nodding, Topac said, "He makes more than trouble. He comes down here, robs the gold of my ancestors and then uses it to lord over us like the conquistadors of old."

Even after hearing the news several times over, Danny still winced painfully when it was confirmed yet again.

Topac took no notice of the bounty hunter's cringe. Instead, he looked over to Ernesto and Lyssa. "You travel with a woman?"

"I'm a reporter," Lyssa said. "I can tell your story to the world and then things will have to change."

"The only way that will change is if someone pulls that Englishman out of his castle," Topac said. "Until that happens, he will keep killing my people and burning their homes."

"I've seen what Farnsworth has done to one village," Clint said gravely. "I won't see that happen to another."

"Which village have you seen?"

"It's a few miles west of here."

Topac nodded. "You mean Santa del Río. Señor Farnsworth burned that down one home at a time. He was kind enough to let the people living there get out rather than burn them along with the rest." When Topac said the word "kind," he spoke it as if it was something vile and rancid from the back of his throat. "There have been other villages where the people were not so lucky."

"How many others?" Clint asked.

"Since Señor Farnsworth has taken over, he's destroyed six villages up and down the river. Those are just the ones I know about. Lord only knows how many have died for him to get where he is today. I hear that Farnsworth killed every last man who knew about the gold that he stole."

"I can vouch for that," Danny said. "Farnsworth has been after me since the moment I got down here. I thought he was just trying to avoid being taken back to the law. Now, I know he was just trying to bury another loose end."

"This can't be allowed to go on," Lyssa said. "This is terrible!" The more she spoke, the more worked up she got. "This is murder and it's happening right out in the open. How can this happen? Something's got to be done about it!"

"Don't worry," Clint said to both her and Topac. "I

don't intend on letting this go on. Not if I have anything to say about it."

"I don't see what you can do," Topac said. "You are only one man. Plenty of men have tried going against Señor Farnsworth, but have only been killed."

"All I can do is try, but you're right about one thing. I can't do it on my own."

"Even the three of you will have a hard time," Topac pointed out. Nodding toward Lyssa, he added, "Sorry. The four of you."

"It won't be the four of us," Clint said. "Not if you can get some of your people together to help me bring Farnsworth and his men to justice."

"You want me to ask my people to put their lives at risk to follow you?"

"No. I want you to ask your people to stand up and fight for their homes."

Topac's expression turned angry. Standing toe-to-toe with Clint, he declared, "We have been doing that already."

"Then you'll have to do it again," Clint shot back. "Look, I don't live here, but I've already seen enough to make my blood boil. I'm not a believer in destiny or any of that, but sometimes a man finds himself in a place where he needs to be. When that happens, he can run in the other direction, sit around and ask questions about it or he can just step up and do what needs to be done.

"I didn't come here for this. I came here because a friend of mine was in trouble and I knew him well enough to know that nobody else would be willing to go three miles to help him, not to mention all the way down into these jungles. Danny Miller may not be a saint, but he deserves one last chance to set his life straight and he sure as hell doesn't deserve to die down here, forgotten by the rest of the world.

"I couldn't live with myself if I let that happen, knowing that I could have done something about it. And I won't be able to live with myself knowing that I just left this place when someone like Farnsworth is running around lighting fires and killing innocent people. I know something about scum like Farnsworth," Clint said. "I may just be your best shot at getting rid of him. I still need some help in doing it, though."

"Some might see that as suicide, Mister Adams."

Clint fixed his eyes on Topac and saw a spark of promise in the other man's face. "Actually, where I come from, they call it a posse. Now how about we start with where I can find him?"

FORTY

Graham Farnsworth had been many things in his life. Starting off across the ocean, he'd been a cobbler's son in a bad section of London. After stealing enough money to pay for the boat trip, he made his way to America, where he started with picking enough pockets to finance his journey west. From there, he'd gone on to bigger and better things.

Murder had always been a part of the bargain. After all, another man rarely wanted to give up his money voluntarily. Farnsworth had taken to killing naturally, but found it to be dirty work. Dirty work was beneath him. That was especially the case now that he was a man of genuine influence.

In his life, Graham Farnsworth had seen many things. Most of those things would cause a simpler man to turn his head in fear or disgust, but Farnsworth looked on with interest at such things. He never got surprised any longer.

That is, until now.

What had once been a quiet plantation house on the banks of the Río Piura was now a compound. It was surrounded by Farnsworth's men and filled with more guns than most forts. Therefore, it was indeed a surprise when

Farnsworth looked out to spot a lone man come strolling
right up along the path leading to the front door.

"Who in the bloody hell is that?" Farnsworth asked.

The man sitting beside him on the front porch swung
his feet down from the rail on which they'd been propped.
The snakeskin boots hit the porch with a solid thump as the
chair beneath him creaked while he leaned forward. "Can't
say," he grunted. "Maybe some beggar?"

"Beggars don't make it through the traps surrounding
this house," Farnsworth snapped. "And they sure as hell
don't make it through the guards that should be patrolling
the grounds. The guards, I may add, that are supposedly
under your watchful eye."

"It's only one man."

"Then get on you feet and greet him, Bakara. Otherwise, I might forget what I'm paying you for!"

Bakara wore a sneer that belonged on the face of a tiger.
Despite the ferocity of his cruel eyes, he made certain to
keep those eyes from looking in Farnsworth's direction.
Instead, he got up and started walking down the path to
meet the new arrival. He stopped the moment he saw who
it was.

"Holy shit," Bakara snarled. "If it ain't the man himself."

Clint stopped with the jungle to his back and Farnsworth's
castle directly in front of him. The description of the house
wasn't too far off the mark. The house was big enough to fit
the bill and had a certain European flair to it that wasn't
found too often in the United States.

"I came for a word with Farnsworth," Clint said.

Bakara squared his shoulders and let his hand drop to
within a few inches of the gun at his side. "You had yer
chance to talk back in Tumbes. All you'll get here is a fight
worse than you had back there."

Looking past the man in the snakeskin boots, Clint fixed
his eyes upon the familiar figure standing on the porch with
his hands clasped behind his back. "You're a wanted man,

Farnsworth. You've stolen a heap of gold that doesn't belong to you."

Clint couldn't help but notice the twitch on Bakara's face at the mention of gold. Farnsworth twitched pretty strongly, too.

"I don't know what you're talking about," Farnsworth said. "Now get off my property before I have you carried off of it."

"Too late for that," Clint replied.

Farnsworth studied Clint for a moment. In that time, several other gunmen had drifted into the area in front of the house. Bakara was whispering back and forth to them in a hurried stream of Spanish.

"Fine," Farnsworth said. "If you want to call me out like some dumb cowboy, so be it." Snapping his fingers, he said, "Kill him, along with anyone else he might have brought with him. I'll pay a bonus of a hundred dollars to the man who brings me the body of this piece of filth who steps onto my property and shows me such blatant disrespect."

Clint stood on that road, thinking the same things that he'd been thinking during his walk from the tree line. At that moment, when he saw the entire plantation come alive with gunman as if they were being spit out from the walls, he realized that he'd been thinking along the wrong lines.

He'd been thinking about the men he'd dealt with and how like them Farnsworth truly was. That might have been true enough, but there was a big difference between those men and the one who'd just snapped his fingers.

Those men didn't have an Incan treasure to fund their own private army.

Clint's eyes widened in shock as man after man came rushing out from where they'd been hiding. There were more places for them to hide than Clint could have seen, especially considering the fact that the jungle itself was something foreign to him.

By the time a few dozen of the gunmen had made themselves known, all of them took up a rallying cry that filled the air. Soon, that became a battle cry. And, a few moments later, gunshots started to rattle within the cry like bolts of lightning shooting amidst the clap of thunder.

Clint's hand was wrapped around his modified Colt before he knew it. He'd even fired a few rounds to cover himself as he made his way back to the tree line, but there was only one thing on his mind as he went through all those motions.

RUN.

Keeping his head low and his feet moving, Clint made it into the trees just as the first bullets started drawing in close to his position. Until then, they'd been hissing through the air over his head, but now they were getting close enough to cause him a bit of worry. When he reached the safety of the trees, Clint could hear the lead tearing through the shelter provided by the jungle.

Danny was waiting for him there, along with Topac. The men were crouched behind a thick pile of logs with their guns drawn. Clint made it there with his chest heaving. The Colt was smoking in his hand as he quickly reloaded.

"Now that was a hell of a plan," Danny mused once he saw Clint was in one piece.

Clint shook his head and snapped the cylinder shut. "Where's Lyssa? Did she get on her way?"

"Sí," Topac replied. "Ernesto and a few of my men escorted her back to Tumbes."

"Good," Clint said after catching his breath. "Now we'll have to see if we can meet her there before getting our heads blown off."

"I told you it was not wise to go there by yourself."

"I know."

"Ol' Clint's used to dealing with men who act like men," Danny pointed out. "Even the lowest dog usually will have a word with a man before taking a shot at him."

"Farnsworth is hardly a man," Topac sneered.

"I see that," Clint replied. "He jumped a whole lot quicker than I expected. Still, I knew he would jump. Are the others ready?"

Topac nodded. This time, he was smiling. "Oh, yes. We have been ready for some time."

"Good. Because it looks like they won't have to wait too long."

Farnsworth's men were charging into the jungle, firing and hollering every step of the way. Even before they caught sight of the blockade Danny and Topac had quickly set up, they got a look at several angry faces staring at them over the barrels of rifles and even from behind bows and arrows.

For a good portion of those hired guns, that was the last thing they ever saw.

FORTY-ONE

The villagers fought like soldiers, every last one of them. Topac had insisted that Clint present his case to them personally if he was going to request their help. He hadn't had a problem doing just that. In fact, all he'd had to do was give them an earnest chance to repay some misery onto Farnsworth for all the damage that had been done and he wound up with a small army of his own.

As Farnsworth's men charged into the jungle, they were already shooting wildly into the trees. This time, however, the trees shot back. A few of the gunmen caught a serious wound, but most of them got just enough to convince them that they were no longer hunting down helpless locals.

After a few of the gunmen dropped, the rest turned tail and ran straight back the way they came. When that happened, the villagers held up their weapons and let out a victorious shout.

"This is a great day, my friend," Topac said. "And it would never have happened without you to guide us."

"You're the leader here," Clint said.

"*Sí*. But after what happened between you and Farnsworth in Tumbes, my people have come to see you as a great war-

166

rior. At least, that is the closest way I can say it in your language."

"Well, tell them to start pulling back into the jungle," Clint said. "I doubt we'll get another bunch of free shots like we just had."

"But we came to help. I can't just—"

Clint stopped him with a hand on his shoulder. "If your men want to help, they can make sure Lyssa gets what she needs. I appreciate what you've done here, but I won't have more of your people get hurt. Just do as I say and fall back to make sure your village is safe."

Before another word could be said, there came another round of gunfire from Farnsworth's plantation house. This time, the shots were more organized and cut a swath through the rows of trees surrounding his property.

"All right," Clint said. "Ask for some volunteers to help divert some fire. The rest of you get the hell out of here. This got hot a whole lot faster than I thought it would."

Topac turned to his people and rattled off a quick string of Spanish. Clint couldn't understand it all, but he knew that Topac was cut off before he could finish. Eight men rushed to Clint's side. Five of them had guns and the other three had weapons that more closely resembled old farming tools.

"Spread out," Clint said to the volunteers. "And shoot anything that moves that comes through those trees. Anything but me, understand?"

Clint looked at each of the faces and got some nods in return. There wasn't any time to waste, so he just prayed that they'd understood the orders they'd been given.

Keeping his head low, Clint ran toward the edge of the tree line. Along the way, he scooped up one of the weapons that had been dropped by one of Farnsworth's retreating soldiers. It was an old Smith & Wesson and filled his off hand rather nicely.

"How much gold are you sitting on, Farnsworth?" Clint shouted. "Fifty thousand dollars worth? Half a million? I'll bet you'll be a rich man, considering how cheap you got all these men."

As he spoke, a few shots were aimed in his direction. Those shots were a fraction of what had been coming a moment ago. Signaling for the villagers to stay down, Clint picked another spot a few paces away and hurried over to it.

"Did you tell your men about the gold, Farnsworth?" Clint hollered. "Or did you just make them think you were already wealthy when you got here?"

His plan had been to walk in and kick up enough dust to put Farnsworth off his guard. Clint also figured on getting a feel for what he was up against, but had quickly discovered the error of his plan the moment he got a look at the number of men guarding the plantation. Now that things had already blown up in his face, Clint decided to do his best to make sure he wasn't the only one to get burned.

The shooting had died off even more. Clint happened to look down at the right moment when he spotted the thin rope that was stretched across what passed for a trail in the dense foliage. As he skidded to a stop, his eyes followed the rope all the way to a thick branch pulled back to one side of the path. That branch was studded with sharpened stakes that would have impaled him nicely had he tripped on that rope.

Topac had warned him about traps like that one. Knowing about them and seeing them were two different things. Luckily, fewer and fewer of the shots were coming. Finally, they stopped altogether. Clint knew better than to think the fight was over, but at least he'd allowed himself one last reprieve before it started up again.

FORTY-TWO

"Is that true, Mister Farnsworth?" one of the gunmen asked.

The Englishman had his own pistol drawn and a murderous look etched across his face. "Is what true?"

"What he said about the gold? Did you really find all that gold?"

Farnsworth twitched and his finger itched on the trigger. He wanted to get back to shooting, but knew that he had to put one fire out before starting another. All of his men were looking at him expectantly. It seemed that some of them had already made up their own minds.

"I've always paid you fairly," Farnsworth declared. "And I'll pay you even more if you bring me the heads of those savages out there."

"What about the gold?"

"Yeah," chimed in another soldier. "What about the gold?"

As it had so many times before, gold fever swept through the pack of greedy men like a plague among a colony of rats. The more they thought about it, the more they talked about it. And the more they mentioned the gold by name, the more they wanted to see it and touch it with their own hands.

"I am in charge here," Farnsworth snarled. "I will not tolerate this . . . this mutiny any longer! Do your jobs and we'll talk about the gold later!"

"So there is gold!"

"Gold!" The cries started rising from the hired guns like smoke from a fire. Soon, they were joined by words that disturbed Farnsworth even more.

"I think I know where it is!"

"I know where he hides it!"

"That's our money, too! Let's get it!"

Farnsworth bared his teeth like a raging animal. "No!" he shouted to the men that were running back toward the house. "Get back here!" When he saw what a lost cause it was to try to talk over the fever that had gripped more than half his men, Farnsworth started shooting at the ones who were storming into the house.

"Goddammit!" Farnsworth screamed. With great effort, he shifted back around to look at the men who hadn't abandoned him. "Bakara! Kill those bastards out there! I don't care how you do it. Cut their heads off if you must. Just kill them all!"

The man in the snakeskin boots smiled. "No problem, Señor Farnsworth."

As Bakara turned to face the men who were still surrounding him, he unleashed a stream of commands given in such a primal growl that the others had no choice but to listen. Even before he was done growling his orders, Bakara was rushing toward the trees with bloodlust gleaming in his eyes. Rather than go against a man like that, the other gunmen charged right behind him.

Seeing that things were well in hand as far as Bakara was concerned, Farnsworth turned his attention toward the plantation home. He ran up the porch and kicked open the door, which was already swinging on its hinges.

"You men want the gold?" he shouted into the house. "You can have it!"

That caused the men inside to stop what they were doing. Some of them were tearing apart floorboards and walls to look for hidden compartments. Others were simply looting whatever they could get their hands on.

"The gold's hidden in the villages we've been visiting," Farnsworth said. "That's why we've been going there. Tear those places to the ground and you won't just find the gold, but you'll have earned it."

One of the soldiers stepped forward. "If we don't find nothing, we'll come back for you." It was obvious in the tone of his voice that his words were no mere threat. They were a promise.

"I would expect no less," Farnsworth said.

"All right, then. After we tear this house to the ground, we start in on those villages."

Farnsworth twitched impatiently. "Fine," he grunted. "If that's the way you want to play it, then here's the deal." He walked past the men who were looting the rooms branching from the main hallway until he made it into a dark-paneled room with a mahogany desk.

A good portion of the men followed him in there, watching as Farnsworth knelt down beside his desk and started pulling at a certain floorboard. That board came up after a bit of coaxing to reveal a small iron door with a combination lock.

Farnsworth twisted the dial to the safe and opened the iron door. He then dipped his hand into the safe and when he pulled it out again, it was filled with gold in all shapes and sizes. There were coins wrapped up in necklaces and even a few nuggets. He stood up, showed the gold to the crowd gathered around him and then tossed the treasure at the men.

"Here," Farnsworth said. "Take this just to know that I mean what I say. You can either try to find the rest of the

gold I have secreted in here or you can work for me a few
minutes more. Do the latter and I'll hand over enough to
make you all rich men."

The hired guns had to think it over for all of two blinks
of an eye. The first of those blinks was just to get over the
sight of all that wealth spilled upon the splintered floor.

"What do you want us to do?" one of the men asked.

"Clear out the jungles of those sons of bitches who
started this fight," Farnsworth said. With every word, his
civil mask dropped away to reveal the monster underneath.
"Help Bakara spill some blood out there and when you
come back, I'll personally split every bit of gold I have
with every last one of you."

"How do we know you won't just run away?"

"It's too late for that. I know I can either get myself
killed by you or those others out there or I can see to it that
we all wind up benefiting from this. After all, isn't this why
we're all here?"

There were a few glances as the soldiers conferred
silently among themselves. After a few muttered words, a
few of them stepped forward to take hold of Farnsworth
while the others started running for the door like a pack of
starving wolves.

FORTY-THREE

Clint made his way carefully back to the edge of the tree line. He could tell there had been another shift in the way things were going, but he couldn't tell whether or not that shift was in his favor. He got his answer soon enough when he heard the roar of all the men who'd charged into the house come storming back out.

They came out in a flood, with guns blazing and fire in their eyes. Before he could decide what to do about it, Clint saw another wave of men come storming into the open. This time, however, the men came out of the jungle rather than the house.

Another big difference was that these men were the villagers that had supposedly gone back to safer ground. Soon, Clint spotted a familiar face among those villagers. That face belonged to Danny Miller, who led the charge like a general trying to overtake an enemy fort.

Guns blazed from both sides as the two groups charged forward.

"Aw, hell," Clint grunted and charged right out to join the party.

Like on most battlefields, the organization within both opposing groups lasted right until they got within striking

173

distance of each other. After that, men started breaking off and fending for themselves. Some of them dropped down with wounds while others tripped over their own feet.

Either way, it was chaos.

Clint spotted one of Farnsworth's gunmen taking aim at a villager wielding a machete. He fired the modified Colt and clipped the gunman's shoulder. That merely brought the gunman's attention toward Clint. Rather than drop his weapon, the gunman spat an obscenity at Clint and took aim. Clint dropped him with one round through the skull.

More and more of the gunmen peeled off from the main group to follow Danny Miller, who was blasting through them like he was impervious to bullets. Danny glanced over to Clint and shouted, "It's about time I got you out of trouble rather that put you into it! Try to get out of here with your skin!"

Before Clint could reply, he lost sight of Danny as the bounty hunter took down two more of Farnsworth's men and bolted into the house.

Several of the villagers were getting hurt and a few of them were in much worse shape. Before he had a chance to think it over, Clint scooped up a discarded weapon and started firing at the hired guns.

"Come on, you stupid assholes," Clint hollered. "I'm the one you're after."

Whether that was true or not, Clint wasn't sure. He did know that the gunmen were just riled up enough to take the bait and come after him as Clint started leading them away from the main group of villagers.

Although it seemed like a whole lot more, there were only half a dozen men who took off after Clint. Thankfully, the villagers took Clint's lead and started falling back into the jungle, as well.

Clint smirked to himself when he heard the gunshots taper off. He smirked again when he managed to get into the jungle surrounding Farnsworth's plantation. That smirk disappeared when he was tackled from behind by the man who'd managed to cut Clint off before he made it another three steps.

Clint punched the man in front of him without looking at his face and kept on running. That distraction was enough to bring the rest of the men closer in to him on all sides. Unfortunately, they all knew the jungle better than Clint.

Perhaps that was why they were all able to avoid the traps that had been set within the trees and the paths winding around them. Clint had been doing a fairly good job, right up until he felt the rope snap around his ankle and his leg get pulled out from under him.

The men who'd been chasing him looked for Clint for a few seconds and talked among themselves. Once they spotted Clint's hat lying on the ground, they thought they'd finally put an end to him once and for all, but Clint used his position above them to unleash a hailstorm of lead that cut down his pursuers like wheat.

Clint's next shot went through the rope that had snared his ankle. For a moment, Clint felt like he was still hanging suspended in the air. Then he realized that he was falling and when the wind started to rush past his ears, it was a split-second before his shoulders slammed against the ground.

If not for the thick layers of roots and leaves covering the earth, Clint might have snapped his neck. As it was, he was able to roll with the impact and right himself while only losing the air from his lungs in the process. Without focusing on the dull pain that accompanied every breath, Clint reloaded the Colt with fresh rounds from his belt.

He snapped the cylinder shut and resumed his course through the jungle.

The river was close. Clint could feel the water in the air and smell it with every breath. It was a mix of rotting plants and the fish that fed on them, but at that moment, it might as well have been the scent of honey and sunflowers.

Clint figured that he could get to the river and make a stand. At least there he would be able to get a look at the men who came at him and he would be past the traps that littered the jungle.

Another few steps and he broke through the trees. The Río Piura wandered nearby and was even wider than he'd expected. In fact, Clint doubted if he could even cross it on foot. To the west, he could see where the river wandered on its way to the ocean. To the east, it meandered back into the jungle and toward the Amazon River.

"Well," he figured while making sure the modified Colt was fully loaded, "this is as good a place as any for a last stand."

That thought was going to be put to the test as the final gunmen chasing after Clint stepped out from the jungle. They looked tired and bloody after fighting their way this far through gunfire and the ravenous jungle itself.

Only one of them had any steam left in his strides as he walked forward and came to a stop a few paces in front of Clint.

Bakara grinned and shook the greasy strands of hair from his face. "I don't know who you are or why you're here," he said. "And I don't even care. All I know is that you caused a lot of trouble here and broke up a nice operation me and Farnsworth worked hard to get going. For that, señor, you will die."

Farnsworth's soldiers weren't the only ones who were tired. Clint felt like a single, walking wound. Every breath he took was a fire in his chest. Every move he made caused some new set of bruises to flare up. Now, he couldn't even take a step without feeling his ankle scream for mercy after having been snared by that rope.

"You want that gold?" Bakara taunted. "You'll have to come through me to get it."

"I don't want any gold," Clint said. "All I want is to put

Farnsworth out of business. I suppose it's too late to bargain now, huh?"

Bakara grunted and shook his head. "There was never going to be a bargain, señor. The jungle is no place for talking."

"No. I suppose it isn't."

Bakara had two other men with him. All the rest had either been picked off by the villagers or had gone back for whatever riches they could scrounge up in Farnsworth's plantation.

Clint stared down each of the three men in turn as they fanned out and planted their feet in the wet soil. All of them already had their guns drawn, but kept their arms hanging at their sides. If they hadn't, each of them knew the shooting would have started a whole lot earlier.

For the moment, Clint forgot about the chain of events that had brought him down into Peru and the mess that had followed. Sometimes, things just turned out that way. All a man could do then was deal with the mess and do his best to clean it up.

That clean-up started when Bakara snapped his gun up and aimed at Clint from his hip.

Clint responded by crouching down while raising his own gun hand up. By the time the Colt was level, he squeezed the trigger and sent a shot into Bakara's chest.

More shots filled the air, but Clint paid none of them any mind. Instead, he calmly looked from one target to another while squeezing the trigger again and again in a methodical rhythm. Although he fired once for every four or five shots that whipped through the air toward him, Clint hit with every single one, while the other men merely wasted their ammunition.

When the last shot split the humid air, the sound of it echoed along the length of Río Piura. The empty Colt felt light in Clint's hand as he straightened up and stepped for-

ward to get a look at the fallen gunmen. Bakara twitched
once before letting out a final gasp. The hole in his chest
looked black as blood poured from his punctured heart and
soaked into his shirt.

The other men kept still, either because they were dead
or figured it was safer to appear to be dead.

Just then, the trees in front of Clint started to shake as
another wave of Farnsworth's hired guns came through.
The fight had been going on so long that the men looked
like wild animals. As soon as they spotted Clint, they ad-
vanced on him.

FORTY-FOUR

Clint knew there was no time to reload the Colt. He knew
he didn't have much of a chance against so many men.
What he didn't know was why the jungle had suddenly exploded and the ground beneath his feet started to shake.

Reflexively, Clint dropped to the mud. On his way
down, he heard something fly over his head that was a
whole lot more than just another bullet. As the screeching
passed overhead, it led to the jungle and ended with another thump and explosion.

When Clint looked up, he spotted the boat coming down
the Río Piura. It had just rounded a bend where it had previously been concealed by the tall trees along the riverbank. A puff of smoke came from the ship's side, followed
by the screech overhead and the thump as a third cannonball found its mark.

Not only were the gunmen no longer advancing on
Clint, but they simply were nowhere to be seen. In fact, a
good portion of the trees that they'd been emerging from
had disappeared right along with them.

Clint got to his feet and ran along the side of the river.
The Gray Crow met him halfway.

"Ahoy!" Captain Layfield shouted from the deck of *The Gray Crow*. "I think you lost something."

With that, Lyssa leaned over the rail so she could wave wildly at Clint. If not for the captain's quick hand, she might have fallen over the side of the boat in her excitement.

Layfield brought the *Crow* to a stop and lowered a rope ladder so Clint could climb aboard.

"I've never been so happy to have a cannon fired at me," Clint said as he tried to catch his breath. "How the hell did you know where I was?"

Layfield nodded toward Lyssa. "We were on our way to pick up some cargo from one of Farnsworth's docks. I was hoping to find that English bastard strung up from a tree, but figured I might as well carry on with business as usual until then. We crossed paths with your lady reporter here, instead."

Lyssa rushed past the captain and practically jumped into Clint's arms. After bombarding him with enough kisses to cover his entire face, she said, "I told Captain Layfield what was going on and he turned around to head this way. We saw some of the shooting going on at Farnsworth's place and were just getting closer when you came along."

"You saw the shooting?" Clint asked.

Layfield's answer to that was to point up at the crow's nest at the top of the boat's highest mast. Since *The Gray Crow* wasn't a full-sized ship, the nest wasn't much more than a barrel strapped to the top of a pole. Only the skinniest of the crew could fit up there without either falling out or tearing the nest down completely.

At the moment, there was one such sailor up there looking toward Farnsworth's plantation through a spyglass.

"Last time we checked," Layfield said, "that house had started filling up again."

"That's not exactly right, Captain," the sailor in the nest

reported. "Those hired guns are rearming themselves. Looks like they're loaded for bear."

"Shit," Clint snarled. "They're probably getting ready to burn down whatever is left of the villages around here. Since they're looking for me, I could probably save some trouble if I just go to them."

Although Clint was ready for Lyssa to try to hold him back, he was a little surprised when Layfield grabbed hold of his shoulder and stopped him dead in his tracks.

"Hold on," Layfield said. "There's no need for that. I think I can end this right here and now."

Before Clint could stop him, the captain was repositioning the cannon.

Farnsworth saw his men coming back to him and couldn't help but smile. There weren't many of them left, but there were enough to get a foothold in the neighboring villages once more. After that, it would be a short ride back to the top of the hill. Who knows? He might just clean up his plantation house and move back again.

Before Farnsworth could get too much farther in his dreams of conquest, the top portion of the house's front wall exploded inward. The moment slowed down to a crawl in Farnsworth's mind since it was something so extraordinary that it bordered on the incomprehensible.

His house simply blew inward as though it were made of straw and toothpicks.

He was still gaping at the hole when the cannonball smashed down into the room where he and a good portion of his most loyal men were standing. After that first one struck, there weren't many left who were healthy enough to see or hear the next salvo hit the house.

The select few who were still drawing breath after that lasted about two or three more minutes. At least, that's how long it took for the house to cave in on them.

FORTY-FIVE

Clint walked back to the plantation house with a few of Layfield's men for support. Along the way, they encountered some of Farnsworth's men. A few of those men were dangling from snares. Some of them were leaning against trees with dazed expressions on their faces and the rest were simply running just to get the hell away from that house.

When he got through the trees and onto the plantation's grounds, Clint spotted another group of men standing and staring at the pile of rubble that had so recently been a house. Topac and his villagers barely seemed to notice when Clint walked up to them.

"Díos mío," Topac said.

Clint took a moment to absorb the destruction Layfield's cannon had caused. "You can say that again."

"Jesus Christ, Clint," came another voice from nearby. "I knew you had some problems with me, but I never thought you'd drop artillery on me."

Clint snapped his eyes over to see who'd spoken and found Danny Miller standing there, smiling back at him. "Last time I saw you, you were headed back into that house. I tried to stop—"

Danny waved off Clint's explanation and flashed a grimy smile. Holding up his hand, he displayed a fistful of gold. "I just went in for some of this. I told you, I'm through chasing bounties."

"I think the locals here deserve that gold more than you," Clint said.

"Go ahead and take it. We've got plenty," Topac chimed in. "Mister Farnsworth stored his treasure like a monkey hiding food. Now that nobody is guarding it, we can dig it up for ourselves."

"You can rebuild your villages," Clint said. "There should be more than enough for that."

"My people will rebuild with our own hands, just the way we built the villages before. The gold will go back to where it belongs."

Danny's grip tightened around the gold in his hand.

"That is yours," Topac assured him. "It's the least we can do to repay you for ridding us of Farnsworth."

Clint and Danny bid their farewells to Topac and his people. A few hours later, they were leading the horses back up the ramp from the riverbank onto *The Gray Crow*.

"I probably should hand over some of this gold to you, Clint," Danny said. "After all, you did come all the way down here to find me."

"Actually, I'll take enough to pay for the trip. That is, since you'll have more than enough to buy some land after you split the money between yourself, Ernesto and Captain Layfield."

Danny winced at that, but nodded. "What about that lady you brought along?" he asked. "Doesn't she get a cut?"

As if knowing that she was the topic of conversation, Lyssa stuck her head out from the door leading below *The Gray Crow*'s deck and motioned for Clint to join her.

"I'll ask her about that later," Clint said as he handed Eclipse over to one of the sailors and followed Lyssa inside.

"You gonna give her that interview now?" Danny shouted after him.

"Yeah," Clint replied as he slipped his hands around her waist. "Something like that."

Watch for

THE GRAND PRIZE

290th novel in the exciting GUNSMITH series
from Jove

Coming in February!

J. R. ROBERTS

THE GUNSMITH

THE GUNSMITH #268: BIG-SKY BANDITS	0-515-13717-0
THE GUNSMITH #269: THE HANGING TREE	0-515-13735-9
THE GUNSMITH #270: THE BIG FORK GAME	0-515-13752-9
THE GUNSMITH #271: IN FOR A POUND	0-515-13775-8
THE GUNSMITH #272: DEAD-END PASS	0-515-13796-0
THE GUNSMITH #273: TRICKS OF THE TRADE	0-515-13814-2
THE GUNSMITH #274: GUILTY AS CHARGED	0-515-13837-1
THE GUNSMITH #275: THE LUCKY LADY	0-515-13854-1
THE GUNSMITH #276: THE CANADIAN JOB	0-515-13860-6
THE GUNSMITH #277: ROLLING THUNDER	0-515-13878-9
THE GUNSMITH #278: THE HANGING JUDGE	0-515-13889-4
THE GUNSMITH #279: DEATH IN DENVER	0-515-13901-7
THE GUNSMITH #280: THE RECKONING	0-515-13935-1
THE GUNSMITH #281: RING OF FIRE	0-515-13945-9
THE GUNSMITH #282: THE LAST RIDE	0-515-13957-2
THE GUNSMITH #283: RIDING THE WHIRLWIND	0-515-13967-X
THE GUNSMITH #284: SCORPION'S TALE	0-515-13988-2
THE GUNSMITH #285: INNOCENT BLOOD	0-515-14012-0
THE GUNSMITH #286: THE GHOST OF GOLIAD	0-515-14020-1
THE GUNSMITH #287: THE REAPERS	0-515-14031-7
THE GUNSMITH #288: THE DEADLY AND THE DIVINE	0-515-14044-9

Available wherever books are sold or at
penguin.com

(Ad # B11B)

GIANT ACTION! GIANT ADVENTURE!

GIANT WESTERNS FEATURING THE GUNSMITH

THE GHOST OF BILLY THE KID
0-515-13622-0

LITTLE SURESHOT AND THE WILD WEST SHOW
0-515-13851-7

DEAD WEIGHT
0-515-14028-7

AVAILABLE WHEREVER BOOKS ARE SOLD OR AT PENGUIN.COM

J799

JAKE LOGAN
TODAY'S HOTTEST ACTION WESTERN!

☐ SLOCUM AND THE BAD-NEWS BROTHERS #302
0-515-13715-4
☐ SLOCUM AND THE ORPHAN EXPRESS #303   0-515-13733-2
☐ SLOCUM AND THE LADY REPORTER #304   0-515-13750-2
☐ SLOCUM AT WHISKEY LAKE #305   0-515-13773-1
☐ SLOCUM AND THE REBEL YELL #306   0-515-13794-4
☐ SLOCUM AND THE SHERIFF OF GUADALUPE #307
0-515-13812-6
☐ SLOCUM AND THE HANGMAN'S LADY #308   0-515-13835-5
☐ SLOCUM AND THE CROOKED SHERIFF #309   0-515-13852-5
☐ SLOCUM AND THE TETON TEMPTRESS #310   0-515-13876-2
☐ SLOCUM AND AND THE SLANDERER #311   0-515-13876-2
☐ SLOCUM AND THE BIXBY BATTLE #312   0-515-13887-8
☐ SLOCUM AND THE RUNAWAY BRIDE #313   0-515-13899-1
☐ SLOCUM AND THE DEADWOOD DEAL #314   0-515-13933-5
☐ SLOCUM'S GOLD MOUNTAIN #315   0-515-13943-2
☐ SLOCUM'S SWEET REVENGE #316   0-515-13955-6
☐ SLOCUM AND THE SIERRE MADRAS GOLD #317   0-515-13965-3
☐ SLOCUM AND THE PRESIDIO PHANTOMS #318   0-515-13986-6
☐ SLOCUM AND LADY DEATH #319   0-515-14010-4
☐ SLOCUM AND THE SULFUR VALLEY WIDOWS #320
0-515-14018-X
☐ SLOCUM AND THE VANISHED #321   0-515-13684-0
☐ SLOCUM AND THE WATER WITCH #322   0-515-14042-2

AVAILABLE WHEREVER BOOKS ARE SOLD OR AT
PENGUIN.COM

(Ad # B110)